THE WITCH WHO TASTED MURDER

PIXIE POINT BAY BOOK 5

EMMA BELMONT

EMMA ONLINE

Emma loves hearing from her readers!

You can contact her at the links below.

Website: emmabelmont.com

Newsletter: emmabelmont.com/newsletter

Thanks!

1

If only Maris Seaver's guests knew what she had to endure for the sake of wine. It was too warm; it was crowded; and it was loud. Somehow the idyllic scene she'd envisioned for the fall harvest of Alegra Winery's Zinfandel crop had not included heavy machinery. Her companion, Rosamel Alegra, had to raise her voice to be heard above the din.

"These were on the vine not thirty minutes ago," the young woman said, pointing to one of the many large plastic containers. It was heaped high and overflowing with long bunches of dusky purple grapes.

Maris guessed that Rosamel was in her late twenties. Olive skinned and short, she wore her long and tightly curled hair in a dark cascade around her shoulders and down her back.

Where she was pointing, a forklift raised the container up some twenty feet in the air, then rolled over to park next to a machine that looked like an enormous cigar. It had to be ten feet long, with a V-shaped hopper at the top. As they watched, the operator rotated the full container in midair, tipping its juicy contents into the big metal V. Hundreds of bunches of grapes, along with some leaves and stems, fell into the machine. Although some of the fruit managed to escape by clinging to the container before falling to the floor, no one paused to pick it up. The forklift was already backing away for the next batch. The pace was almost manic.

Rosamel leaned in and put her mouth near Maris's ear. "That's the crusher," she said.

A couple of men in rubber aprons and boots quickly adjusted the location of the enormous metal pan underneath it. Though the aroma of freshly picked fruit was thick, the wide waterfall of juice that now splashed into the pan filled the air with a new scent that was sweet and spicy at the same time.

"Amazing," Maris said, almost shouting. "From the vineyard to juice in under an hour."

Rosamel nodded. "Let's step outside." She pointed to the front of the cement room and headed that way.

Maris followed her through the cavernous opening into the dirt yard just beyond. Outside, the vineyard proper was only yards away. Acres upon acres of vines spread out in every direction. On what had to be one of the last warm days of the season, the sun blazed down from a powder blue sky to the heated soil.

As she and Rosamel neared the immaculate rows of plants, the young woman came to a stop and turned back to the winery. The bustle of the harvest was finally far enough away to talk.

"We do the sorting out here," she said, pointing to a conveyor belt.

A half-dozen men and women stood on either side of it, hands and arms flying, picking out mostly twigs and clumps of leaves, but also the occasional cluster of grapes. They simply tossed the unwanted material to the ground. The fruit that made it through sorting was dumped by the conveyor belt into one of the large containers at the end. On the other end of the belt, a small tractor brought over a long cart full of stacked crates. As Maris watched, the forklift went to work again, lifting each crate and dumping it on the moving belt.

"It's not what you thought," Rosamel said. "Is it."

Maris had to laugh. "Not quite." Images of plump peasants in bare feet who were happily stomping grapes in giant wooden vats would have to be banished.

"It's a business," the young woman said.

"And quite a successful one," Maris observed, "judging by the number of employees." There had to be twenty or thirty people sorting and crushing. She gazed out to the rolling vineyard with its lush green plants as far as the eye could see. Who knows how many more people were in the fields?

Now it was Rosamel's turn to laugh. "A lot of these wonderful folks are volunteers."

Maris frowned and looked at her, and then at the sorters. They were sweaty and filthy and working a mile a minute. "You're kidding."

Rosamel shook her head, smiling. "Nope. It's a time-honored tradition. We'll be feeding them and I can guarantee you that the wine will flow." She nodded toward the conveyor belt. "We've got volunteers who've been with us for ten years running." The young woman crooked up one dark eyebrow. "It helps when you win awards."

"Ah," Maris said, nodding. In essence, that was also why she was here. Alegra Winery had been producing gold medal winners since their first release ten years ago. She had made them a staple at the B&B, her go-to wine, which was the reason for her visit today. She bought by the case. "It would seem that nothing succeeds like success."

Yet something about Rosamel and the winery's amazing achievements felt like more than know-how and elbow grease. If Maris wasn't mistaken, something a bit magical might be at work as well.

Rosamel lowered her voice. "We even have a buyer for this year's releases."

Maris regarded her. "A buyer?"

The young woman nodded, her mass of dark curls bobbing. "He wants the entire release."

Maris stared at her. "Wait. Are you saying he wants to buy everything?" She glanced at the conveyor belt and all the containers waiting to be poured onto it. "And it has yet to be made into wine?"

Rosamel grinned at her. "You've got it."

"Every varietal?" Maris asked, still trying to wrap her head around a purchase of that size. She gestured to the scene in front of them and then the surrounding vines.

"The entire release," Rosamel confirmed.

Maris's eyebrows rose as she went through the numbers in her head. Hundreds, maybe thousands, of bottles of wine that were yet to be made were already spoken for. It had to be hundreds of thousands of dollars worth of wine.

"A single buyer wants it all?" Maris asked, still a bit incredulous. "Even if you drink a bottle every..."

Rosamel shook her head quickly. "Oh no. I'm sure he'll sample it, of course. But it's an investment. He'll sit on it for...who knows how long." She lifted her shoulders and hands. "Ten years? Twenty? Fifty?" She crossed her arms over her chest, watching the volunteers sorting. Another giant container of grapes was dumped on the belt. "He'll let go of a few cases here, a few cases there, a few at auction."

"Wow," Maris said. It was like buying artwork, or maybe stocks.

"It's an investment," Rosamel said again, "and a smart one, even if I do say so myself." She gave Maris a little elbow. "But don't worry. I'm going to set aside your usual purchase at your usual price. The deal hasn't been cinched yet."

Maris's eyes widened. "*Thank you.* I appreciate that."

The young woman nodded to her. "You're very welcome. We local folk gotta stick together." She glanced back to the winery. "Speaking of which, shall we go back to the tasting room? I'm sure today's purchase will be ready by now."

As they headed back toward the crushing room, Maris said, "Thank you very much for the tour as well—especially at this busy time of year. It's been incredibly interesting."

Rosamel waved a hand. "My busy time is over, thank goodness. Now that the harvest is almost all in, it's up to my father to make the wine. He's the one who'll–"

Despite the cacophony of the machinery, loud voices rose above it. When Maris looked over, a young man at the crusher was being grabbed from behind by an older man, who had him by the collar.

"Oh no," Rosamel muttered, heading in their direction.

2

Maris quickly followed Rosamel as she trotted over to the two tall men, even as the other workers backed away. The forklift operator pulled up short of the crusher in order to keep from hitting the older man, who was dragging the younger one backward. Without another trough of grapes to crush, someone turned off the loud machine.

"Harlan!" Rosamel shouted.

The younger of the two men looked over at her immediately, followed by a glare from the older man. "She knows your name?" he demanded.

Not only tall but obviously fit, Maris had no doubt that the bearded younger man could have easily deflected his attacker, and yet he didn't. In fact, it seemed he was taking care not to hurt the older man. As Rosamel neared them, he simply peeled the older man's fingers from the back of his collar.

"Harlan," Rosamel said, "what are you doing here?"

The young bearded man put his arm across the older man's chest, holding him back. "Isn't it obvious?" he said, smiling at her. "I'm helping with the harvest."

"You're what?" both she and the older man said.

"We have our own harvest!" the man shouted, and Maris heard just the tinge of a German accent. "What is the matter with you?" He slapped the back of Harlan's head, making Maris blink. One of the workers gasped. Rosamel shrieked just a tiny bit and covered her mouth.

But Harlan seemed not to have noticed as he continued to smile at her. "Rosamel, I'd like you to meet my father, Friedrich Krone." Harlan looked over his shoulder. "Father, this is Rosamel Alegra."

Some of the surrounding workers re-peated the man's last name in hushed whis-pers—and Maris knew why. Friedrich Krone was the owner of the nearby Crown Winery, the first winery established in the region. Though Maris had heard of him, she'd never seen him. But as she gazed at the two men now, she could see the resemblance. Though Friedrich was thicker around the middle and only wore a mustache, she could see traces of his auburn hair among the white. It was exactly the same color as Harlan's. Both men were equally tall, but they clearly shared another characteristic, the ice blue eyes.

"Your father?" Rosamel said, looking between the two men.

Maris heard the conveyor belt outside fall silent, as some of the volunteers peeked inside the crushing room. Rosamel stared open mouthed at Friedrich, as he gaped back at her.

Harlan looked over his shoulder. "It'd be polite to say hello."

His father's mouth turned down as he scowled at his son. But when he glanced back at Rosamel, his brows slowly rose. "All these months," he said, as understanding seemed to dawn. "Now I see why you have been sneaking around."

Despite her olive skin, Rosamel decidedly

blushed. Then she glared at Harlan. "Why didn't you tell me you were volunteering?"

"Why didn't you tell *me*?" Friedrich yelled. The older man grabbed him by the collar again. "Volunteering for the enemy," he grumbled, tugging him backward.

The enemy, Maris thought. For decades Crown Winery had enjoyed an uncontested pre-eminence in the area. But not only had their holdings been dwarfed by those of Alegra, their sales had as well. Although Maris hated to see one of the older businesses in the area falling behind and fading away, she had to admit that she liked the Alegra wines more. Not only that, but she had the comfort of her guests and the reputation of her B&B to consider. As with all things related to her property, she had to give it her best effort. No one had ever complained that the wine she served at the evening wine and cheese was too good.

Friedrich tugged on his son's collar. This time Harlan didn't resist. As he walked backward, he gave Rosamel one more smile and a little shrug. But in return, she gave him a bleak and pained look. As father and son disappeared around the corner, Maris found herself watching Rosamel, along with everyone else. It took her a few moments to realize she had their undivided attention.

The young woman cleared her throat. "The grapes aren't going to crush themselves," she said, her voice strained.

Although several of the outside volunteers exchanged looks, someone started the conveyor belt again. The forklift operator continued on to the crusher, and someone turned it on. Maris quickly covered her ears.

Rosamel turned to her and shouted, "Let's go see about your wine."

3

As Maris followed Rosamel back into the winery, she couldn't help but wonder about Harlan Krone and his helping a rival winery at harvest time. His father had obviously been upset, and both he and Rosamel had clearly been surprised. Though Maris would have liked to have questioned the young woman about him, her quick stride, stiff back, and sudden silence made it clear she wasn't in the mood for talk. As they made their way back up the arched brick tunnel, Maris almost had to trot to keep up. Though they passed other winery employees as they emerged from the branching passages, Rosamel didn't greet them as she had earlier. Instead, she seemed to be trying to melt the floor with her glare.

"Thank you for the behind-the-scenes peek," Maris finally said. "It was very kind of you to take the time."

As though she'd just remembered that Maris was there, Rosamel jumped a little but recovered quickly. "Totally my pleasure," she said, mustering a smile. "It's busy, but that's what makes it a good time for a tour. Otherwise we'd just be looking at barrels."

Back in the wine tasting room, the crowd had grown considerably. Several of the staff in their long-sleeve, button-down winery shirts, were busy pouring samples for the happy visitors. Plenty of snacks were on hand as well: pretzel sticks next to jars of mustard; slices of cheese next to water crackers; bagel chips accompanied by a lox and whipped cream cheese spread. In her twenty-five years in the hospitality business, Maris had visited many tasting rooms, but Alegra Winery's was particularly generous. Certainly they could afford it, but Maris also knew that it paid off in two ways. Not only was the tasting room known for its food, it helped the visitors not to imbibe on an empty stomach.

Of course, the star attractions of the room were the long wooden tasting counters. The tops, built on wine barrels, gleamed with a high polish. There was, however, no place to sit, undoubtedly by design.

"Here we go," the young woman said as they approached the large counter at the end of the room. Two cases of wine marked with Maris's name sat just in front of it. "Your wine is ready." Rosamel rounded the end of the counter to stand behind it. "I'll have someone take that to your car. But before that, what can I pour for you?"

"Try the chardonnay," said someone at the counter next to her.

Maris turned and recognized the young man, though they hadn't had much opportunity to talk. "Mr. Gorian," Maris said smiling. "How nice to see you here."

Tall, blonde, blue-eyed, and immaculately groomed, Charles Gorian was the image of young success. Maris put his age at thirty and his wealth somewhere in the hundreds of millions. Today's gray suit with royal blue shirt and matching tie were as dapper and well tailored as yesterday's. No doubt his fire-engine red Bentley SUV was parked outside. Although Maris had recognized his

Rolex, she'd never known that Bentley even made an SUV.

Rosamel put a white wine glass on the counter in front of Maris. "Charlie, I didn't know that you knew Maris."

Charlie flashed his brilliant white smile. "We've only just met. I'm staying at her lovely B&B." He raised his wine glass to Maris. "And please call me Charlie."

"How kind of you to say, Charlie," Maris said, as Rosamel poured the chardonnay. She pointedly looked at his glass. "You've already discovered one of the treasures of Pixie Point Bay."

Charlie laughed a little, a warm and pleasant sound. "Oh I discovered Alegra Winery some time ago." He swirled the wine in his glass, brought it to his nose, and inhaled deeply. "It's the reason I'm visiting the area." He took a sip, swishing it around in his mouth before swallowing. Then he eyed his glass. "The 2015? I didn't think there was any left?"

Rosamel took on an overly cagey look, and shifted her eyes from side to side before regarding him. "If you're interested, I might know a guy who knows a guy."

Charlie laughed. "I need to know that guy." He lifted a tote bag from the floor near his feet. "In fact, I've brought that guy a little gift." He set his glass down and, with a bit of a flourish, brought out...a bottle of wine.

Maris cocked her head at it. Charlie had brought a gift of wine to a winery? Wouldn't that be the last thing that–

"Oh my goodness," Rosamel gasped. "I can't believe it."

Maris looked at her, and then at Charlie, who seemed as pleased as Rosamel was surprised. He grinned back at her, his blue eyes sparkling. "Think he'll like it?"

Maris took a closer look at the bottle. Dusty in spots, its label was yellowed with age as well as stained. The red foil covering the cork was wrinkled. But then she saw the year of the vintage: 1947. Her eyebrows rose.

"Father is going to go absolutely nuts," Rosamel gushed. "A Cheval Blanc 1947 St-Emilion? I don't think he's ever seen one."

Charlie nodded. "Good. Because today he's going to taste one."

Rosamel's mouth dropped open. "You're going to open it?"

"A little gift," the young man said. "From

me to the finest vintner I've ever met, not to mention the man's amazing palate. I can't think of anyone who'd appreciate it more."

A winery employee came up behind Charlie. "Mr. Gorian," the man said. "Mr. Alegra will see you now."

Charlie downed the rest of his glass. "Excellent." He put the aged bottle back in the tote bag. "Good to see you, Maris." He winked at Rosamel. "I'll be back."

As they watched him depart, Rosamel gave a low whistle. "That's going to knock Father's socks off."

"I take it that's a well known wine?" Maris asked.

Rosamel took a deep breath. "I'd say legendary. At auction, it'd easily go for a cool $25,000."

Maris had to do a double take. "That bottle? The one he's just carrying around in a tote bag?"

"Yep," the young woman answered, still watching Charlie as he disappeared through a door at the other end of the room. "A rare and exceptional Bordeaux, to say the least." She moved Maris's glass closer to her. "I'd say he's really intent on getting the new release, as if I didn't already know that."

Maris stared at her. "Charlie Gorian is your wine investor?"

"Yep," Rosamel replied.

"He's so young," Maris whispered.

"Started tasting and collecting when he was in college," Rosamel said. She fetched a notepad and pencil from a small wooden box on the counter. "Wine is how he made his millions."

Maris took the tasting notes pad, but paused. "He *made* his fortune in wine?" She picked up her glass. "I didn't know such a thing was possible."

Rosamel smiled and gave her a little shrug. "I guess it is now."

As Maris tasted the chardonnay, she made a few notes. It had a citrusy flavor that was on the bright side. She could easily imagine it paired with a semi-soft and mild goat cheese. When she finished, she said to Rosamel, "Charlie was right. That was most definitely worth tasting. Really wonderful."

"Thank you," Rosamel said. "A gold medal winner that year."

Maris had already noted from the young woman's conversation with Charlie that this particular vintage was no longer available, but it was nice to taste just for the sake of comparison.

Rosamel leaned in. "I might be able to find you a bottle," she whispered.

Maris smiled at her. "That would be terrific."

Rosamel nodded. "I'll be right back." She pulled over a tray of pretzel sticks and mustard before she turned and headed to the other end of the counter and then out through a back door.

As Maris dipped a pretzel into the brown mustard, so full of seeds that the pretzel could stand in it, her cell phone rang. She fetched it from her purse and saw that Cookie was calling. Sometimes the chef of the B&B would add something to Maris's shopping list while she was out. But since the wine and cheese hour was Maris's purview, Cookie rarely had any requests when it came to the wine. Maris frowned a little as she answered.

"Cookie," Maris said into the phone, "I didn't leave the trash in the hallway, did I?"

"No," said the chef. "I wouldn't have

called about trash." There was a pause. "It's Claribel."

Maris went still. The lighthouse, also affectionately known as the Old Girl, was a magical being whose name was Claribel. In her hundred-plus years of service, her beam had never once failed. Even the fire in the conical tower hadn't stopped her.

"What happened?" Maris asked, already finding her keys.

"She's blinking," Cookie told her. "In a southerly direction."

Blinking, Maris thought. The only time she'd seen that was when she'd been at an art gala in the Towne Plaza. An art critic had later been found murdered. Here at the winery, there was no direct line of sight to the lighthouse, nor did Maris think the beam would be visible at this distance.

"She's blinking?" Maris asked. "Here?"

"Yes," Cookie said. "I was out in the greenhouse and saw the beam go on and off. I just wanted to make sure you were all right." There was silence again. "So, are you?"

"Oh yes," Maris quickly assured her. "Just tasting wine and making notes." She glanced around the room. The happy visitors were enjoying the wine and food, and nothing seemed at all amiss. "Everything here is fine."

"All right," Cookie said, sounding relieved. "Just make sure it stays that way."

Maris smiled. "Will do. I'll be leaving soon."

"Good," the chef said. "I'll see you for lunch."

As Maris hung up, she thought about the crushing room. Though father and son had certainly been at odds, Claribel wouldn't have signaled for that. No, her warnings were about life or death. Maris glanced around the tasting room again. Everyone here seemed happy. She gazed out one of the windows. A wink from the Old Girl toward the south covered a lot of ground.

"Everything all right?" Rosamel asked.

Maris turned to find that the young woman had reappeared carrying two bottles of wine. She set them down on the counter. But before Maris could say anything, the same man who'd come to fetch Charlie ran into the tasting room and directly to Rosamel. Most of the conversations in the room stopped as he dashed past them.

Rosamel frowned and stared at him. "What is it?"

The man was breathing hard and tried to swallow. "It's Dominic," he gasped.

Rosamel stared at him. "Father?"

The man nodded repeatedly, his face pale and sweaty. "Yes, yes, your father." He tried to swallow again and Maris almost poured him some wine. He grasped the edge of the counter with both hands, and looked Rosamel in the eye. "In Cellar 14. I think he's dead."

4

As Rosamel sprinted through the tasting room, Maris ran after her. They hurtled down into the arched brick corridors of the winery's vast and labyrinthine storage rooms. Chamber after chamber of barrels and bottles, stacked floor to ceiling, flew past until Maris finally saw the room numbers—twelve, thirteen, fourteen. Rosamel came to such an abrupt stop that Maris nearly ran into her back.

"Father?" the young woman gasped.

Over her shoulder, Maris could see the man. He was sprawled face down on the stone floor with what looked like a wound to the back of his head. Without thinking, Maris pushed past her into the room and then put a restraining arm in front of her.

"Stay here," she said.

Maris ran to Dominic Alegra's side, knelt, and put two fingers to his neck, just under the jaw.

Nothing.

She moved her hand slightly, and tried again.

"Father?" Rosamel whispered.

Maris tried one more time, repositioning her fingers, but there was no pulse. Nor was he breathing. The only thing she felt was her stomach plummeting. Dominic Alegra was dead.

Careful not to disturb the body—and averting her eyes from the back of his head—Maris stood and backed away. When she turned to Rosamel, the young woman's hands were clasped over her mouth and her big watery eyes stared into hers.

Maris slowly shook her head.

"No!" Rosamel shrieked, and started toward the body with her arms outstretched. "Father!"

But Maris easily intercepted her. "Rosamel," she said, "don't look. Please." She held the shorter woman back, even as she burst into sobs. "I'm sorry," Maris said, hugging her.

For several moments, it was all that Maris could do not to sob herself. Such a sudden death was a shock to the system, and the last thing she would have anticipated. But as Rosamel's whole body shuddered with the intense crying and gasping for breath, Maris did her best to comfort her. Only then did she finally realize where they were: underground.

A freezing cold shiver of fear shot down her back.

She'd run after the young woman without thinking. They'd run down countless corridors, turning this way and that. It hadn't occurred to her that they were going beneath the surface of the ground. There wasn't a window for many yards in any direction.

Maris kicked herself. Of course wine was stored in subterranean cellars. That's where the temperature was cool and stable. But it was also where her claustrophobia kicked in.

She broke out in a sweat.

It's not an elevator, she said to herself. *It's not an elevator.*

Being trapped in one for hours had created her fear of enclosed spaces—all those years ago. Since then, she'd managed to pick and choose the places that might trigger a response, mostly choosing to stay away. Now was definitely not the time for a full-blown claustrophobia attack.

Rubbing the young woman's back, she said, "Rosamel, we need to call the police."

But the poor thing couldn't stop sobbing. Maris wasn't even sure that she'd been heard, but she could hardly blame her. The death of her father was dreadful in itself, but the scene in the cellar was unnerving. But as Maris waited for the young woman's weeping to subside, a familiar anxiety began to build in her chest. If she hadn't been steadily working on searching through the B&B's basement, she'd likely have run from the room already. She was doing well but she couldn't wait forever.

"Rosamel," she said gently, grasping her by the shoulders and separating from her. "Listen to me. We need to call the police because...I think your father might have been killed."

The young woman's eyes widened and she stared at her. "Killed?" she managed to say through her tears. She swiped at her eyes and looked over to where her father lay.

Maris turned her away from the sight. "Yes," she said firmly. Rosamel was bringing her crying under control. "We need to get the police here as quickly as possible."

"Killed?" she said, as though the word didn't make any sense.

"I hope I'm wrong," Maris told her. "But if I'm not, then every second counts. We've got to call the police."

"The police," Rosamel echoed. She sniffed and swiped at her eyes again, as she took her cell phone from her back pocket. "No service." She looked up at Maris. "Not down here."

"Then we have to go up," Maris said, guiding her toward the door. Only then did she realize that two winery employees stood just outside the doorway, both wide-eyed and staring at the body: a young woman that Maris didn't recognize and the pasty-faced man who had come to tell Rosamel what he'd found. "Everyone out," Maris said to him. "Clear everyone out of the cellars." To the woman she said, "Call the police. Tell them there's been a murder."

5

———

Maris waited on a bench next to the large circular drive of the winery. The mid-morning sun was a brilliant, bright yellow, and a light breeze wafted through the colorful plantings that lined the curved sidewalk. The mission style architecture of the winery gave it a rustic and historic feel, with its terra cotta walls, red tile roofs, and even a bell tower. But Maris knew that it had been designed from the ground up with every modern convenience and the latest technology, including a state-of-the-art restaurant that was often used to host wedding receptions and corporate events.

Arms stretched out along the bench's

back, she closed her eyes and lifted her face to the sky, soaking up the warm rays. The experience of light and air helped to dispel the last of the lingering tension from her brush with an unexpected enclosed space. She took in a deep breath that carried with it a hint of lavender from the flower borders, and Maris used it to focus. In moments, the authorities would arrive and she would lead them back down to the cellar. Now was her chance to replenish the feeling of being outside and without bounds. As though she could store it, she inhaled deeply again and slowly let the breath go—just as a siren in the distance alerted her to Mac's arrival.

Slowly she opened her eyes. The sheriff's white SUV turned the corner into the circular drive, followed by the coroner's van. The siren died and Maris stood up, smoothing out her skirt. Both of the vehicles parked at the top of the circle, directly in front of her. She could already see the sheriff's surprised look.

"Maris," he said, as he got out. "I didn't expect you here."

Sheriff Daniel "Mac" McKenna was tall

and moved with the easy grace of an athlete. His slate gray eyes focused on her as he came around the car.

"I didn't expect to be greeting you here either," she said, smiling. "But here we are."

He mounted the curb and stood in front of her. As usual, his khaki and brown uniform was perfectly pressed, and the gold sheriff's badge glittered on the breast pocket.

He smiled back at her. "Here we are indeed." He glanced at the winery. "Buying wine?"

She nodded. "Exactly. I was here making my usual purchase for the B&B, and also getting a tour of the harvest operations."

"Did you discover the body?"

"No. One of the employees did. I just happened to be with the deceased's daughter when she got the news."

The coroner joined them, a man that Maris recognized but had never met. His young male assistant trailed behind.

"Mr. Voight," Mac said to the coroner. "May I introduce Maris Seaver? She's the owner of the Pixie Point Bay Lighthouse and B&B."

Voight looked to be in his early fifties, his jet black hair graying only a little at the temples, but with deep furrows in his forehead and around his mouth. His piercing dark eyes appraised her.

Although Maris smiled and held out her hand, the man ignored it. "No, you may not," he said to Mac. "I understand there's a body."

Maris's smile vanished and she dropped her hand. Mac gave the man a raised eyebrow, and the assistant in back of the coroner rolled his eyes.

"You understand correctly," the sheriff replied coolly. "Maris will be showing us the way."

The coroner looked at her, his expression bland. "Then show us."

Feeling heat rise to her cheeks, Maris turned on her heel and strode off, not bothering to see if they were following. Mac trotted to get ahead of her and opened the front door to the winery. She led them directly into the tasting room, where a few visitors were still milling and being served by the winery staff. As though she were leading a parade, Maris marched through, with Mac once again opening the door in front of her that led to the cellars. The floor immediately began to slope downward, but she ignored that and focused instead on her anger. She heard the footsteps behind her echoing from the vault of arched bricks as she silently seethed and counted off the cellar numbers. Finally at number fourteen, she simply stepped aside and gestured to the interior.

Mac gave her a little smile as they entered. Mr. Voight followed him, staring straight ahead. His assistant gave her a sheepish grin, before disappearing inside. She followed, a few paces behind.

"Maris," Mac said, as the coroner bent over Dominic Alegra. "Has the body been disturbed?"

She shook her head. "Not to my knowledge. Rosamel and I rushed...down here as soon as she received word."

Though she'd stumbled on the word 'down', she was determined Tasted not to dwell on it. Instead she focused on the coroner and his assistant. While Voight crouched next to the body, the young man took something that looked like an oversized digital thermometer from the toolbox he had opened.

"Blunt force trauma to the back of the head," Voight said.

At that moment, there was a noise behind Maris. She turned to see the forensics team enter—the same two women who had investigated Reggie Atkinson's death. They politely nodded to her as they went by.

"Estimate for the time of death?" Mac asked the coroner.

He looked up from his notepad. His assistant showed him the digital readout, and the coroner noted it down. He scribbled something quick. "One to two hours." He looked up at the sheriff and pointed to the back of Dominic's head. "I'll know more after the autopsy, but I can tell you right now that wound appears to be concave."

"Curved inward?" Mac said, stepping closer for a look.

The coroner indicated the rows upon rows of bottles.

As the various investigators went about their jobs, Maris unfortunately had a moment to reflect. She'd moved further into the cellar than she'd realized. Silently, she took a small step backward, then another. Though the room was cavernous, it was darker than she remembered. Though she called up the memory of being outside and the smell of lavender, it didn't do much to alleviate the slowly rising tide of uneasiness that was beginning in the pit of her stomach.

Maris was thinking of excusing herself when the older of the two forensic investigators said, "Sheriff, take a look at this."

She motioned him over to a red stain on the floor. Maris grimaced at it as Mac crouched down, examining it closely. "What is it?"

"Wine," the investigator said, and Maris breathed a sigh of relief. "Not too surprising given the surroundings, but this spill is fresh."

She had gestured to the large wooden shelves that surrounded the entire room. Each one was filled with dark green bottles that sat in holders at a slant. In fact, as she took a moment to try and calmly observe, she saw that the room extended at least a hundred feet to the right, with many rows of similar shelves retreating into the distance, under more dim lights.

Dominic Allegra was lying near a couple of upright barrels that were in the middle of a clear expanse on the stone floor. Unlike the rest of the cellar, bright modern lighting hung from the ceiling casting a wide spotlight around him. There were four wine glasses on the one barrel, and a clipboard with paper on the other, as though they were used as tables. Though the rising anxiety of the enclosed space had begun to tighten in her chest, Maris looked at the four glasses, each of which had just a hint of red wine in its bottom.

"'They quaffed away at the best the cellar could afford,'" Mac muttered.

"Burns," said Voight, without looking up from where he was making notes on the tablet.

But the phrase reminded Maris of something. "Charlie Gorian was bringing a bottle of wine to Dominic as a gift," she said, making all heads turn to her. "He's a guest at the B&B and Rosamel and I ran into him in the tasting room where he was waiting for his meeting." She nodded at the wine glasses. "That might account for at least two of the glasses."

"Interesting," Mac said, standing and

glancing around in all directions. "Bringing a gift? I don't see an open bottle."

Like him, everyone else swiveled their heads around, except for the coroner, who was hard at work.

"But it might be anywhere," said the younger of the two women. "With all these bottles…"

"It was old and dusty," Maris said, "a 1947 vintage."

But the investigator only shrugged. "We'd still need to find it among all these, where dust isn't exactly in short supply."

The sheriff looked at Maris. "This guest of yours, Gorian, is he still here?"

Maris saw her opportunity. "I don't know but I can go back up to the winery and check." She turned to leave.

"I'll go with you," Mac said. He turned to the older of the two investigators. "Do you have some fingerprint cards and a pad that I can borrow?"

"Sure," the woman said, and she went to a bright orange tackle box and opened it. Maris watched, wondering if she was purposefully moving at a glacial speed. Finally the investigator handed the materials to Mac. Again,

Maris made to leave, but he paused next to the coroner.

"When forensics is done," the sheriff said, "you're free to remove the body."

Voight didn't look up from his tablet. "I know."

6

____

Once they were in the long corridor, Maris took the lead, heading up to the front of the winery at a good clip while trying not to draw attention to that fact.

"Don't mind Voight," Mac told her. "That's just his way."

"The way of rudeness?" she said. "I think he's mastered it."

Mac laughed a little. "He's all about the job. Super focused. It's part of what makes him good at what he does."

"I'll take your word for it," she said.

Up ahead, light spilled in from the entrance to the main corridor. The tightness in Maris's chest began to ease and she took a deep breath. She slowed down her pace as well.

"Do you know where Rosamel Alegra and Charlie Gorian are?" Mac asked.

"If he's anywhere, I imagine Charlie is in the tasting room," Maris said, considering for a moment. "Rosamel... I'm afraid she was in a bit of shock. She may have gone home." Except that it was harvest time, and the head vintner was dead. "Or not." As they exited the main corridor into the wide lobby that bordered the tasting room, Maris said, "Let's ask one of the staff." They went to the counter where a receptionist in the standard button-down shirt waited.

The sheriff took the lead. "Can you tell me where I can find Rosamel Alegra?"

The young woman—who might have been Alegra's age—grimaced a little. "I think she's in Mr. Alegra's office." She paused and then added, "Is it true? Is he dead?"

Mac exchanged a look with Maris, then turned back to the receptionist. "Yes. I'm afraid he is." He glanced at the various doors that branched off from the lobby. "Where is Mr. Alegra's office?"

She pointed to the one at the far end. "Through there, first door on the right."

"Thank you," Mac said.

Rosamel had gone to her father's office, Maris thought. Had she already taken the helm?

Behind the door that was marked off-limits to the general public, they found a set of offices that was nothing short of stupendous. The wide wood paneled corridor led to several workspaces but the first was magnificent. Through the open door they could see that the entire far wall was glass, with a view of the spreading vineyard almost as far as the eye could see. The big room even had its own patio, with a table flanked by two rows of chairs. Rosamel sat in one of them, at the end of the table with a box of tissues.

She looked up as Maris and Mac entered, her eyes, red and puffy, focused on the sheriff. As they passed through the office to the patio, Maris noted the enormous roll top desk and the framed set of gold medals that hung above it. A bookcase next to it was full of binders, with the spines labelled with dates. The sideboard on the far wall was stocked with bottles of wine, glasses, corkscrews, and napkins. Casual leather chairs clustered around a low brass table. The vintner's office was the size of a small apartment.

As they exited through the sliding glass door to the patio, Rosamel stood.

"Ms. Alegra?" Mac asked.

"Yes," she said.

He extended his hand. "Sheriff McKenna. Please accept my condolences on your loss."

Although she shook his hand, she looked at Maris. "Then...he really is dead."

So Rosamel had yet to come to terms with the fact that her father was dead, let alone take control of the business.

Maris nodded and gave her a sympathetic look. "Yes, Rosamel. I'm afraid it's true."

The shorter woman released Mac's hand and sat down hard. "Oh god," she muttered. Although Maris thought she might burst into tears again, she only hung her head, shaking it. "I can't believe it."

"Ms. Alegra," Mac said pulling up a chair for Maris. "I'm afraid I've got to ask you some questions." Maris took a seat as Mac fetched a chair for himself. "I know it's a difficult time, but the sooner, the better."

The young woman lifted her head and straightened her back. "Of course," she said, with some resolve in her voice. "I agree. The sooner, the better."

Mac sat down and took the notepad from his shirt pocket. "Your father, Dominic Alegra, was the owner of the winery. Is that true?"

"Was," Rosamel whispered. Then she focused on Mac. "Yes, he owned and operated it."

"And when you say operate you mean…"

"He was the vintner," she said, glancing at his office through the glass. "He was responsible for…" She shrugged a little. "Well, for making the wine." She looked back to the sheriff. "He picks the time for harvest based on the grapes' acidity and sweetness. He adds the yeast and sugar to start the fermentation. He decides on the barrels and when the wine is ready for them. He makes the decision on when to bottle." She shook her head as her expression became bleak. "There's just so much," she muttered.

"And your job?" the sheriff prompted.

She tried to smile, but not too successfully. "The non-winemaking." She gestured to the rows of vines. "Taking care of the vine-yard, staffing, equipment, marketing...and stuff like that."

"That's quite a lot," Maris said.

Rosamel shrugged. "I started in the tasting room, like everyone else. That was ten years ago."

Mac nodded, as he finished jotting down a note. "Was your father on good terms with everyone here?"

"Everyone," she said quickly. "Everyone loved him." She smiled a little. "He pretended to be a curmudgeon but everyone saw through that." She tilted her head at the winery. "Ask around."

"I'll do that," Mac said. "And your relationship with him?"

Her eyes teared up. "I adored him," she declared, as her lower lip began to tremble. "He was all I had. He was everything."

Maris brought the box of tissues closer and Rosamel took one, putting it to her already red nose.

"Is there anyone," Mac said, "who might have wanted him dead? Anyone at all that you can think of?"

She shook her head, and sniffed. "Absolutely no one." She paused and looked at him. "So, he was...killed?"

Mac nodded. "It definitely looks that way."

The young woman shut her eyes as though she had a sudden headache. "Gods. Who would want to do such a thing?"

"At this time of year," Maris said, "at the harvest, it seems as though there are a lot of people at the winery."

Rosamel blew her nose and nodded. "They're everywhere. It's controlled chaos —barely."

"Who would have reason to be in the cellars?" Mac asked.

"No one," she said. "Not really. Not yet anyway. Only the vintner."

"All right," Mac said. "Who would have had access?"

The young woman took a deep breath and blew it out. "Everyone. We don't keep the doors inside the winery locked. People are always coming and going."

"Are most of them familiar to you?" Maris asked. "As in return volunteers?"

Rosamel nodded. "Yes." She went still,

and then looked at Maris. "Oh my god, I'm going to have to tell them."

Maris gave her an understanding smile. Although the news had likely already shot through the entire facility, it was true. Rosamel would need to say something.

"I'd be glad to help you," Maris said.

Though she appeared to think about it for a moment, she finally shook her head. "No. That's all right. It ought to come from me." She heaved a heavy sigh.

"Are you the head of the winery now?" Mac asked.

Rosamel blinked. "I...I guess I am. I didn't think of it like that."

"And I assume you inherit all your father's assets, as well as the responsibilities?"

Though his tone had been non-comital, Rosamel bristled nonetheless. "I don't know what you're trying to imply, and I don't even know the answer to your question. He set up the corporation, not me."

"Fine," Mac said. "There's just one more thing." He brought out the small fingerprint card and pad that he'd borrowed. "I'll need to get your fingerprints."

Rosamel's eyes went wide. "Mine?" she said, putting a hand to her chest. "Why?"

"To eliminate them from the crime scene," Mac said calmly. "It's strictly *pro forma*. It'll take a couple of minutes." He put the card on the table, and opened the ink pad. "I'll start with your right hand thumb."

As he finished with the thumbprint, Rosamel looked at Maris. "We were together. You told him that, right? We were together all morning."

Maris smiled at her. "Yes, of course. I've told the sheriff everything. Truly, this is just so the team can *ignore* your prints."

Rosamel seemed to relax. "Okay," she muttered.

They all sat in silence for the rest of the printing. When he was done, Mac took out a business card and handed it to her, along with a packaged towelette to wipe her fingers. "If there's anything else that you might remember that you think would be relevant, please don't hesitate to call me."

She took the items in both hands, staring down at the card. "What's going to happen now?"

Mac sat back, tucking his notepad away

in the shirt pocket. "The coroner is going to perform an autopsy, and Cellar 14 will be off limits until the forensics team is done with it." As he stood, so did Maris. "Again, my sincere condolences on your loss, Ms. Alegra."

Maris looked down at the young woman, who was now gazing at the table. Her expression seemed lost. "This was his favorite spot," Rosamel whispered. She looked out at the vineyard. "He could sit here for hours, next to the vines, with a bottle of wine, some pasta, and me." She pushed herself away from the table and stood.

Maris touched her arm. "Would you like me to stay?"

Rosamel turned and covered Maris's hand with her own. "No, but that's kind of you. Thank you. I think I'd better go see the staff and volunteers." She glanced at the table. "He would have wanted the harvest to go on."

"We'll see ourselves out," Mac said.

Rosamel tucked his card into her back pocket, proceeded into the office without a backward glance, and then headed back into the winery.

As she and Mac eventually followed, Maris said, "It's a task that I don't envy her."

"Nor I," the sheriff agreed, glancing after her. "It's a lot for such young shoulders." After a moment, he asked, "Did you know Dominic Alegra?"

Maris shook her head as they entered the large lobby. "I've always dealt with Rosamel. I'd never even met him, just seen him in passing."

Mac nodded as he came to a stop. "This Charlie Gorian, the fellow with the gift bottle. Is he still here?"

Maris paused. "Honestly, I don't know. The last time I saw him he was going to meet Dominic." Then an idea occurred to her. "But I know how we can tell." She pointed outside. "His car."

As they made their way to the parking lot, Maris relished the feel of the sun on her skin.

"You know what kind of car he drives?" Mac asked.

Maris nodded. "It's kind of hard to miss." She scanned the large lot. "A fire-engine red Bentley SUV."

Mac shielded his eyes against the bright

light and looked in every direction. "Nothing like that here."

"Then hopefully he's at the B&B," Maris said.

The sheriff took out his keys. "I'll meet you there."

7

On the drive back to the B&B, Maris would normally enjoy the beautiful countryside. But today her eyes were on the rear view mirror. Mac had decided to follow her. Although he kept well back, there was always something about being followed by a law enforcement vehicle. She glanced between the mirror and the speedometer every few seconds. Normally her Type A+ personality would have had her speeding from one locale to another. But now she had to grin at herself. It was probably the safest she'd driven in a long time.

As she rounded the final curve in the coastal approach to the lighthouse, she breathed a sigh of relief. Even at this distance she could see that the bright red SUV was parked in front. Of course, she'd hate to be leading Mac on a wild goose chase but, more than that, she didn't want to see a suspect simply disappear.

As her tires crunched over the manicured gravel of the long drive that led down to the B&B, Maris also noted that Bear's truck was here as well. Their bigger-than-life handyman had his hands full when it came to the Victorian property. If the lighthouse wasn't in need of maintenance, then there was usually something in the large adjacent lightkeeper's house—which now served as the bed and breakfast—that needed his attention.

Maris never tired of driving up to her home. The many red-roofed gables of the two-story white structure were vivid and cheery. The lighthouse rose up behind it, its conical tower a matching white. The optical room at the top glittered even from this distance. Beyond both lay the azure waters of Pixie Point Bay, and the ocean beyond that. Despite the predictable good weather, the scene itself never seemed the same.

Maris parked and got out, waiting for Mac, who parked alongside her. As he got out, he eyed the red Bentley. "That's quite the car," he said. The dove gray leather interior trimmed in red was beautiful and Maris realized that the back seat wasn't a bench, but two more bucket seats instead. The entire thing looked as though it'd just rolled off the factory line. The sheriff gave a low whistle. "A couple hundred grand at least."

Maris stared at him. "I'm sorry. Did you say a couple *hundred* grand?"

"Oh, easy," he said, turning away from it. He took the fingerprint kit from the passenger seat before locking the doors. "Mr. Gorian does well for himself."

As they made their way to the front door, Maris said, "Rosamel told me that he made his fortune through wine investing. In fact, he was meeting with Dominic to make a rather large purchase."

Mac opened the door for her. "Hence the gift of wine?"

As she preceeded him through the door, she nodded. "A gift that apparently could fetch $25,000 at auction."

"Hmm," Mac said, closing the door. "Maybe even a gift worth killing for."

She regarded the sheriff. That hadn't occurred to her but it was true. At first glance in the cellar, it was nowhere to be seen.

"Let's check the public rooms first," she suggested. But a quick trip through the living and dining rooms, as well as the library, parlor, and kitchen revealed that no one was downstairs. Through the vestibule that led to the back porch, Maris could see Cookie, the B&B's chef, in her herb garden. There was no sign of Charlie anywhere. "Upstairs we go."

Until tonight, when two couples would be arriving, Charlie was their only guest. Unsurprisingly, his was the only door that was closed.

"If you'll permit me?" Maris said, and Mac stood back. She knocked lightly on the door. "Charlie? It's Maris Seaver. May I have a word?"

There was an immediate "Yes?" and then some sounds of movement and finally footsteps. Maris took a step back as the door opened. Though Charlie was wearing the same shirt and slacks, he'd obviously just thrown them on. His feet were bare and his blonde hair was rumpled, as though he'd been sleeping. Although she'd clearly woken him up, he was smiling—until he saw the sheriff.

"Maris," the young man said. "What can I do for you?"

"Actually," she said, "it's not really something you can do for me. This is Daniel McKenna, the Medio County sheriff. I'm afraid we have some bad news, and a few questions."

"Oh," he said blinking. "Oh, okay." He opened the door wider. "Please come in."

As expected, the bed looked slept in, and the rest of his clothes had been tossed onto the back of the embroidered chair.

"Sorry to disturb you, Mr. Gorian," Mac said.

"No worries," Charlie said. He grabbed his clothes off the chair and tossed them on his open suitcase. "Would you care to have a seat?"

The sheriff put the fingerprint kit on the dresser. "No, thanks," he said, taking out his notepad.

"I'm fine," Maris said.

Charlie stood as well. "You said you had some bad news?" He looked between the two of them, his brow creased.

"Yes," Mac said. "Earlier today, Dominic Alegra was found dead."

As usual, Mac had provided the minimum of information and Maris also noted how closely he was watching Charlie. But the young man's reaction amounted to...nothing. Instead, he simply looked at Mac, and then at her, his face blank.

But as she watched, his brows slowly drew together.

"Dominic," Charlie said, nodding slowly and just once. "Alegra," he said, drawing out the syllables. His eyebrows flew up, and he staggered back a pace. "Dominic Alegra?" The color drained from his face. "*Dominic Alegra?*"

Before he fell down, Mac quickly stepped forward, took him by the arm, and sat him down in the chair. Maris went to the bathroom, filled a glass with some water, and brought it back.

"Impossible," the young man muttered. His blue eyes searched Mac's face. "But that can't be." Though Maris held out the water to him, he didn't seem to see it. "Is this some sort of joke?" he demanded. He shot to his feet, but teetered. "If this is some kind of joke–"

"I can assure you, Mr. Gorian," Mac said sternly, "I did not drive out here for the sake of a joke. Dominic Alegra is dead."

Like a marionette whose strings had been cut, he sat right back down.

"Drink this," Maris told him.

He blinked up at her, and then down at the glass. He took it in both shaking hands, and managed to drink some. Then he set the trembling glass in his lap. He shook his head and stared down into the water.

"I can't believe this," he whispered. "I was just with him." Then he jerked his head up, staring at her. "What happened?"

Maris looked at Mac, who said, "He died under suspicious circumstances. But you say you were with him?"

"Suspicious...?" Charlie whispered.

"What time was that?" Mac asked.

The young man stared at him. "I don't know," he said faintly, then cleared his throat. "It was this morning. I had an appointment at ten, but he was running late." He thought for a moment, then looked at Maris, pointing at her. "You were there. I saw you in the tasting room." He looked at the sheriff. "She was there."

"Right," Maris said to Mac. "But I didn't note the time."

"It had to be a little after ten," Charlie said. "I didn't have to wait long."

Mac jotted down a note. "What was the nature of your meeting?"

"I was there to buy wine," he said, his voice a bit more firm. "We were finalizing the deal."

"And did you?" Mac ask.

"Finalize the deal?" the young man asked. Then his face fell. "Only on a handshake."

"Tell me about your meeting," Mac said. "Be as detailed as you can."

Charlie took a deep breath. "Well, I went down to the cellar—I don't remember which one—and met him there. He was logging some observations when I came in." Charlie paused for a moment, then nodded to himself. "I talked about purchasing this year's release and we went back and forth on price." He shrugged. "But not much. We both knew what it was worth. After we shook on it, I brought out the 47 St-Emilion." He smiled a little at Maris. "I showed it to you in the tasting room."

"Yes, you did," Maris agreed. "Did you open it?"

Charlie scoffed. "He could hardly wait." Then he grinned a bit sheepishly. "Well, really, neither of us could." He paused again, as if savoring that moment. "It was exquisite. We'd just had our first sip when Friedrich Krone barged in."

"Friedrich Krone?" Mac asked.

"The owner of Crown Winery," Charlie told him. "He was spitting mad about something."

Maris recalled how upset Rosamel had been about him in the crushing room.

"And then what happened?" Mac asked.

Charlie shook his head and shrugged. "He saw the 47 St-Emilion and stopped in his tracks. It's a once-in-a-lifetime bottle. We all knew it." Then he looked from Mac to Maris and back again. "But let me tell you what an amazing man Dom was. He actually offered Friedrich a glass." He looked at them both again. "Can you believe it?" It sounded like Charlie was the one who couldn't believe it. "It was an amazing moment. Everything I'd ever heard about it was right." He smiled sadly as he gazed down at his glass of water. "I'm glad Dom got to taste it."

"And where is that bottle now?" Mac asked.

Charlie gazed up at him, with a little smirk. "He let Friedrich take the last of it." He shook his head slowly. "What a class act, what an amazing vintner, and what an incredible palate."

"So Friedrich Krone barges in on your meeting," the sheriff said, "apparently angry about something, but then has a glass of wine and leaves with the bottle?"

Charlie nodded. "That's what a 47 St-Emilion will do to you." Mac frowned a little as he made a note, which Charlie apparently saw. "Ask Friedrich. He'll tell you the exact same thing." He glanced at Maris and then back to the sheriff. "If there's one thing that vintners can come together about, it's wine."

"How much longer were you there?" Mac asked.

"Not long at all," Charlie said. "We were done, the St-Emilion was gone, and Dom was busy. I left a few minutes after Friedrich."

"And about what time was that?" the sheriff said.

Charlie paused for a few moments before grimacing and shaking his head. "I really don't know. I'm not very good with time."

Mac nodded. "When you left the winery, where did you go?"

The young man looked at his bed. "I came right here," he said. "I think that big guy in the overalls saw me."

"That would be Bear," Maris said. "Bear Orsino is our handyman," she said to Mac.

Charlie sat back in the chair. "I still can't believe it."

"Just one more thing," Mac said, putting away his notepad. He picked up the fingerprint kit he'd set on the dresser. "I'll need to get your fingerprints."

Now the young man sat forward again. "Mine?"

Mac nodded, removing the card and pad. "Just standard operating procedure, Mr. Gorian. If you don't mind, that is?" When Charlie shook his head, Mac set the card on the dresser. "If you could come stand here, please."

For the next few minutes, Charlie

watched in seeming disbelief as the sheriff took his prints. When he was done, Mac gave him a business card with the usual request for any more information.

"Also, if you could stay in the vicinity until I've completed my investigation," Mac said, "that'd be appreciated."

Maris already knew that Charlie was booked for an extended weekend.

"I can do that," Charlie said, but then paused. "As long as it's not too long?"

Mac nodded. "That's my goal."

8

Back downstairs, Maris said, "Mac, if you have a moment, would you care to join me for a cup of coffee in the back?" She glanced at the ceiling and lowered her voice. "It's more private."

"Sure," the sheriff said. "That sounds good."

"I'll meet you out there," she said, smiling.

In the kitchen, she filled a cup from the vacuum carafe, put it on a saucer, and skipped the creamer and sugar. Mac took his coffee black. When she came out onto the porch, he took the coffee from her.

"Smells great," he said. "Thanks." He took a sip. "Ah, perfect as always." He turned to the herb garden where Bear was helping

Cookie bring a tray of small plantings from the greenhouse to her garden. "I see you've made an addition," he said pointing to the greenhouse. "Looks good."

"Thank you," Maris said. "All the credit goes to Bear. He built it from the ground up—literally from the paving stones of the floor to that nice hatch opening near the top."

"A talented man," Mac said. "It really seems to match the historic buildings."

"He does so much of the maintenance and fixing," Maris said, "that I think it's seeped into his bones. Cookie mentioned having one, and the next thing we knew, it was done."

"Hmm," the sheriff said, gazing at it. "I'm going to keep that in mind. My property isn't historic but a good handyman is hard to find."

Mac had hardly ever mentioned his personal life. Maris didn't even know where he lived. "Well, I can highly recommend Bear."

The sheriff gazed at her. "Of course your handyman and the greenhouse aren't the private conversation that you wanted to have."

"Right," Maris said. Though she'd be

happy to stand at the railing all day chatting with him, she also wanted to add what she'd observed. "When Rosamel was giving me a tour this morning, I saw Friedrich Krone too."

"Oh?" Mac said, taking another sip.

"While she was showing me the crushing room, he exchanged angry words with a young man there. Then he grabbed the guy, who was his son, and hauled him away. I had the distinct impression that Rosamel and Harlan knew each other. Afterwards, she was quite upset."

"What were the Krones doing in the Alegra crushing room?" the sheriff asked.

"It looked to me like Harlan had pitched in with the various volunteers there to help with the harvest."

Mac frowned, turning away from the garden. "Isn't it harvest time at their winery too?"

Maris nodded. "That's exactly what Friedrich told him before he grabbed him by the collar and dragged him away."

Mac was silent for a few moments. "I think that dovetails pretty well with what we just heard from Mr. Gorian." He took another sip of coffee. "It would seem he was still irate when he went down to the cellar."

"But, from what Charlie said, I don't think anything was resolved," Maris noted. "It didn't sound like there'd been an argument, or even a discussion." Then an idea occurred to her. "I wonder if he came back later."

"Good question," Mac said, finishing the coffee. "One that I'll put to Mr. Krone when I see him." He set the cup back in its saucer. "I have a question for you as well."

"Shoot," she said, wondering if there was anything that she'd left out. But a strange look came over Mac's face. He stared at his feet for a moment before he looked at her and continued. "I was wondering if we might have lunch sometime." He held up a hand. "Unrelated to any investigation."

Maris felt a small zinging thrill shoot up her spine. With his mysterious gray eyes, salt and pepper hair, and broad shoulders, Mac was easily the best catch in Pixie Point Bay, and likely far beyond.

"I think that would be wonderful," she said, all smiles.

But before they could talk about a date or a time, the chime of his cell phone interrupted the moment. He took it from his utility belt, as Maris took his cup and saucer from him.

"McKenna," he said, then listened. He glanced out at the ocean, then nodded. "Got it. On my way," he said. "ETA in twenty-five."

Maris smiled at him. "Duty calls."

He nodded. "It literally does." He clicked the phone back into its holder, and smiled at her. "But we've got a plan for lunch, details to be determined. Agreed?"

"Agreed," she said, feeling that little zing again. "And I won't let you forget it."

9

After Mac saw himself out, Maris turned back to the view of the garden and the bay beyond it, already looking forward to their lunch date. She smiled as she reached down to pick up Mac's saucer and cup, only to see it vanish.

Maris froze.

The inner vision of her magical talent—precognition—took over.

At first alarmed by her ability, she'd eventually accepted it and now even looked forward to it, particularly when there was a murder case. She took in a slow breath and waited as an image coalesced.

The vineyard of Alegra Winery swam into view, much as she had seen it today, the rows of vines stretching across the sunny landscape. But rather than the many volunteers harvesting among them, Maris saw Rosamel —by herself. The young woman looked down at the ground and seemed to be wandering, perhaps lost in thought. Though it made sense, given the loss of her father, it didn't appear to Maris to reveal much about the man's murder. As she pursed her lips to consider it, the vision winked out.

"Huh," she muttered, as the cup and saucer reappeared. "Rosamel alone among the vines."

That's not where Dom had been killed, but was it a clue to the murderer's motive? Their identity? Even their location? As usual, the brief view of the future left more questions than it answered. But at this point, Maris knew to simply trust it. It would eventually come in handy.

As she picked up the chinaware, she thought of lunch again—but not with Mac. She realized she was hungry, so she headed out into the garden.

"Hey, you two," Maris said to Cookie and Bear.

The diminutive older chef looked up

from where she was compacting the soil around a new plant. Ruth "Cookie" Calderon had been the chef at the Pixie Point Bay lighthouse and B&B for decades. Though her shoulder length hair was now more salt than pepper, it seemed that her love of gardening and cooking must be keeping her young. As far as Maris knew, she'd never missed making the breakfast buffet and her garden seemed to be growing by leaps and bounds.

"How was the winery?" she asked, brushing the hair from her face with the back of her gloved hand.

"Um, not too good," Maris replied. She recounted the tour of the harvest, the tasting room, and finally the discovery of the body.

"How dreadful," Cookie said lowly. She shook her head and grimaced. "Poor Rosamel. It has to be awful for her."

"She was devastated," Maris agreed. "But I think it's actually a good thing for her to have the harvest to deal with."

"Keeps her busy," Cookie agreed.

"Is that why the sheriff was here?" Bear asked.

A head taller than most men, he was easily two heads taller than either herself or

Cookie. He wore his hair cropped short but sported a full beard, kept nicely trimmed. While Maris's gift was precognition, and Cookie's was making potions, Bear was a shape-shifter.

As usual, he was wearing a short-sleeve white t-shirt under the blue bib overalls that stretched around his bulging middle. In one hand he held Cookie's trowel, and in the other was a new planting in a small pot. Both seemed like miniatures in his big hands.

"Yes," Maris told him. "I'm afraid so. It turns out that our guest, Charlie Gorian, is a wine investor and was meeting with Dominic before he died."

A man of few words, Bear only responded with, "Hmm."

But to Maris, that seemed to size up the situation pretty well. There were simply too many unknowns at this point. Charlie had seen Dom this morning, but so had Friedrich Krone—and that only accounted for three of the wine glasses.

"Exactly," she agreed. She regarded the two of them. "But as horrible as Dominic's death is, I actually didn't come here to talk about the winery. I'm going to head into town and pick up lunch. Any ideas?"

Cookie looked up at her big companion. "How about if you make the call this time, Bear?"

"Me?" he said, as he touched the trowel to the front of his bib making dirt fall from it. His bushy eyebrows arched high.

"Why not?" Maris asked, grinning at him.

"It isn't always up to us," Cookie said. She put her hand out for the trowel, which he gave back to her. "The sooner Maris leaves, the sooner we eat." She held out her other hand for the plant, which he also handed to her. She took them both and moved over a foot before beginning to dig a small hole.

For a moment, Bear watched her and stroked his beard. Then it was as though a light came on behind his eyes. "Delia's Smokehouse," he said. "It has been awhile."

Maris nodded. "Great choice," she said, turning back to the house. "We have menus inside."

"The crab sandwich," he said, stopping her.

Maris turned back to him, smiling. "Crab

sandwich for the big man," she said. "Cookie?"

Without looking up, the gardener simply said, "Same."

"Me three," Maris said, nodding. "I'll be back in a jif."

10

Though Delia's Smokehouse had undergone a name change since Maris's childhood, the woody exterior with its many windows remained the same. To her it had always seemed like a cross between a log cabin and a classic diner. But the one thing that she could always count on was the luscious, smoky aroma that emanated from it. Maris smiled as she stepped inside.

There was a good lunch crowd today. The simple wood chairs that flanked the long, roughly hewn plank tables were almost all full. Even the counter at the left only had a few stools available. At the far right a couple of lunch-goers were circling the wood and steel salad bar, filling their plates. Above the big room hung a giant wagon wheel lit with electric candles.

"Well, I'll be peppered," Eugene Burnside said, coming to the hostess podium with some menus. "Maris Seaver. It's been a month of Sundays, hasn't it?"

Likely in his late seventies, Eugene's round face certainly didn't show it. His rotund form moved easily as well, like a man decades younger, and bright red suspenders held his pants in place. With his white mustache curving up and his hazel eyes smiling, Maris decided it wasn't his looks that belied his age. It was his attitude. Eugene had to be the most positive person she'd ever met.

She grinned back at him. "It sure feels that way. How are you, Eugene?"

"Busier than a one-armed paper hanger, enjoying my daughter's cooking a bit too much, and awful glad to see you." He handed her a menu. "How about you?"

"The lighthouse beam keeps shining," she said smiling, "I've been enjoying Cookie's breakfasts way too much, and I'm glad to be here." Although she already knew what she'd be ordering, she took the menu anyway.

Eugene's face uncharacteristically

sobered. "Did you hear about Dom Alegra?" he asked.

Maris nodded with a grimace. "I did. In fact, I happened to be there."

Eugene's eyes crinkled as he stared at her. "You were?"

She recounted how she'd been there to make her usual wine purchase for the B&B and how Rosamel had given her a tour. Finally, she told him of how the morning had ended.

"Poor girl," Eugene said. He pointed to the wine display at the end of the counter, full of Alegra wines. "We're customers too." He shook his head. "I think Dom would have wanted her to continue the family tradition, but young people these days." He shrugged. "I guess they have to go their own way." But as he regarded the restaurant and then looked back at her, he smiled broadly. "I'm a lucky man. Delia is carrying on our tradition. I really don't know what more I could ask for."

"Well, I couldn't agree more," she said. In essence, that's what she had done as well, taking over the B&B and lighthouse when her aunt had died.

"I'm guessing that you didn't come here so I could tell you how wonderful my daughter is," he said. "You already know that." He winked at her. "What can I get for you today?"

"I'd like to get four crab sandwiches," she said, giving him the menu. "To go, please."

He nodded to her and put the menu away. "Coming right up." Then he headed to the kitchen, pausing at a couple of the tables as he bussed some plates and refilled some glasses of water.

Maris contented herself with watching the Towne Plaza out the front windows. The picturesque center of Pixie Point Bay was ringed with Victorian homes, most of which had been turned into businesses. Their pastel colors glowed under the midday sun. In the center of the trimmed grass stood the brilliant red gazebo designed in an elaborate Oriental style. A number of tourists seemed to be out, a mirror of the busy restaurant.

"Here you go, Maris," said a bubbly voice behind her.

Maris turned to see Delia Burnside, a plump and curvaceous red-head with perfect ivory skin. Even if she hadn't known that

Delia was Eugene's daughter, the inner light of their hazel eyes would have been a dead giveaway.

"Four crab sandwiches," she said, setting down a recycled lettuce box on an empty bench in the waiting area. Inside it were the four sandwiches, and also four bottles about the size of sodas.

"What do we have here?" Maris asked, peering down.

"I don't think you've ever sampled our own homemade and world famous hot sauces," Delia told her.

Maris looked at her. "You're absolutely right, since I didn't even know you made hot sauces."

Delia nodded, causing her bright red curls to bob. "Oh yes, world famous," she said again. She pointed to the bright label of each one in turn. "Delia's Smoldering Smokehouse is mild. Delia's Sizzling Smokehouse is medium spicy. Delia's Searing Smokehouse is hot. And Delia's Scorching Smokehouse is what I call nuclear." She grinned at Maris. "It's dad's favorite."

"Well, how delightful," Maris said. She hadn't grown up with spicy food, but had definitely learned on the job. The many local cuisines around the world in the hotels where she'd worked had been one of the few plusses to that career. She'd first learned of Thai food in Bangkok, and authentic Mexican cuisine in Cabo San Lucas. Visiting the same types of restaurants back home it had sometimes shocked her at how different the meals were made in order to cater to more local tastes. In the end, everything here was considerably less spicy, even if it looked the same.

Maris glanced down at the bottles. "I'm looking forward to trying them. What do I owe you?"

Delia gave her the handwritten bill. "The hot sauce is on the house. But I'd really like to know what you and Cookie think."

Maris took out her credit card and handed it over. "Well, that's awfully kind of you, Delia, but I'm very happy to pay."

Delia swiped the card and typed in some numbers on the machine. "Nonsense. Please just give me your honest feedback on them. That'll be payment enough."

As Maris signed the credit card slip, she said, "Thank you. I appreciate that." She put away the card, tucked the receipt into the box, and picked it up. "I'm sure our guests will be delighted to sample them as well."

"Oh," Delia said, pretending to be surprised and doing a poor job. She smiled. "Well, if your guests have any feedback I'd be doubly glad." She grabbed a few paper menus from under the podium and dropped them into the box. "Just in case," she said and gave Maris the same exact wink that Eugene had.

Maris nodded as Delia held the door open for her. "Absolutely, and thank you."

11

"Hot sauce?" Cookie said, sounding alarmed. "At the breakfast buffet?"

Bear was eating his second sandwich but stopped in mid-chew as his big brown eyes flicked to her face.

Maris had arrived home with the box from Delia's and brought everything to the back porch, noting that Charlie's Bentley was gone. Hopefully he'd managed to calm down and gone out, either to eat, or maybe even get some sunshine and fresh air. As usual, the B&B guests were on their own for lunch and dinner—unlike the occupants or their handyman.

They'd all dug into the sandwiches straight away, and it was Cookie who'd noticed the various bottles. Although Maris had been excited for the guests to sample them, apparently that opinion wasn't universally shared.

"Not necessarily at breakfast," Maris said carefully. "I was thinking more the Wine Down."

Although the evening wine and cheese didn't particularly lend itself to pairings that involved hot sauce, Cookie was clearly not interested in them appearing at the morning buffet.

"The breakfast buffet is designed as a whole," Cookie said, putting down her sandwich. Bear put his down as well. "The flavors are meant to compliment one another, not compete, or get drowned out."

Maris held up a hand. "My mistake," she said quickly. "I meant the Wine Down, of course. The buffet is perfect as is." She eyed Bear.

He nodded as he swallowed his last bite. "Perfect."

Cookie sniffed as she picked up her sandwich. "Well, I wouldn't call them perfect, but I do try." She regarded her lunch. "Speaking of which, Delia makes a mean crab salad sandwich."

When she took a bite, Bear picked up his sandwich and did the same. Then a thought occurred to Maris. She reached over to the box and selected one of the bottles.

"Perhaps they'd go well with Delia's food," she suggested.

She'd picked Delia's Smoldering Smokehouse, the mild sauce. The label was brightly colored, and Maris recognized not only the illustration of the smokehouse, but a cartoon version of the sauce's namesake. In her slightly comedic caricature form, Delia was smiling and holding a saucepan that looked like it was on fire.

With a little twist of the plastic red cap, Maris opened it. Then she gave it a sniff. There was definitely a vinegar base to it, maybe some garlic, and definitely red peppers. But the aroma was much more complex than just those ingredients and Maris suspected there were several spices involved as well. She shook out a few drops on her plate, as Cookie and Bear watched. Then she dabbed her finger in the little puddle and tried it on the tip of her tongue.

A burst of flavor with just a hint of heat blossomed and spread in her mouth. Having become a fan of spicy food, Maris analyzed the flavor. It almost reminded her of the hot sauce she'd had when she'd worked at the resort in Bali—what was its name—Sambal. Delia's sauce had just a touch of the grilled shrimp paste and lime juice that had given the Indonesian sauce its special tang but the chili was different.

She sprinkled a few drops on the crab salad of her sandwich and took a bite. Her eyes narrowed and she nodded to Cookie. Covering her mouth she said, "It goes *perfectly* with this sandwich."

Cookie smiled at her. "Good. But I'm a bit of a purist, so I think I'll have mine without."

Bear, however, picked up a different bottle from the box. "Delia's Searing Smokehouse," he read. "Hot."

Although the background of the bright label seemed the same, the image of Delia was slightly different. Though she was still smiling, she held a saucepan in one hand, and two in another, all with flames rising from them.

As he twisted the cap off, Cookie warned him. "Be careful with that, young man."

Maris nodded. "That's the third hottest and, judging from the mild, that might have a pretty good kick to it."

The bottle looked too small in his meaty hand as he shook out several drops onto the crab salad and bread. When he set the bottle aside, Cookie and Maris exchanged a quick look, then watched as he took a bite.

"Mmm," he said grinning as he chewed. But then his brow furrowed. "Mmm?" Pink rose to his cheeks. "Uh oh," he mumbled. As his face turned red, he put the sandwich down. Beads of sweat popped out on his forehead. He looked around him and then jumped to his feet. With a speed Maris hadn't expected for his size, he raced down the steps of the porch and ran to the garden hose.

Cookie chuckled a bit as he drank what appeared to be a few gallons of water. Maris reached to the box and turned the two remaining bottles around to see the labels.

"You've got to wonder about the nuclear version," Maris said. She showed it to Cookie. "Apparently it's Eugene's favorite."

Cookie gave her a wry smile. "Fire elementals. They could probably eat a five-alarm chili and not bat an eye."

"Fire elementals?" Maris asked.

"I've always suspected as much," Cookie said. "Witches who can control fire. They've got a pretty high tolerance for heat." She nodded at the hot sauces. "In any form."

"Including fire?" Maris asked, blinking.

Cookie nodded. "Fire, smoke, spice. They thrive on it."

Maris sat back in her chair. Delia's Smokehouse. It made so much sense. No wonder Eugene's daughter followed in his footsteps. Cookie pointed to the bottle that she still held.

"Be careful with that," the chef said. "If you open it, make sure to wash your hands afterward. And whatever you do, don't touch your face or eyes."

Maris quickly put the bottle back. "No problem, since I don't think I'll be opening it."

Cookie wrapped up the rest of her sandwich and sat back, patting her flat stomach. "I think that's all I can eat, but it was wonderful. Thank you for picking these up."

Although Maris could easily have polished off the second half of her sandwich, she gazed down at her tummy. Though she'd managed to drop a few pounds since returning to Pixie Point Bay, she had some ways to go before she was near a normal weight for her height. She wrapped up her sandwich too. Years ago she'd been told if she wanted to be thin, then she should stick with a thin person and do what they do. Maris had noticed that, despite being a chef, Cookie ate sparingly, and she never said she was 'full.'

"These will make for good leftovers," Maris said. As she got up, she put the two half sandwiches in the box, along with all the bottles of hot sauce. "I'll put the sandwiches in the fridge."

Cookie looked up at her. "I'll wait for our young man to finish his lunch." They both looked toward the garden where Bear was fanning his mouth, before drinking more water. "Assuming he can."

As Maris took the leftovers through the vestibule and into the house, she thought about Eugene and Delia. He'd said that he hoped Rosamel would follow in the family tradition, the way Delia had in theirs. Did that mean that the Alegras shared some magic ability that had to do with their business?

But before she could ponder it further, a tiny, tinny harmonica-like meow drew her attention to the floor in the hallway.

"Mojo," Maris said, smiling down at her fluffy black cat. "Where have you been?"

His big amber eyes looked up at her and he meowed again. Then he turned and trotted to the dining room. But at the threshold he paused, looked over his shoulder at her, and meowed again.

She was being paged.

12

In the dining room, Maris set the box of leftovers and hot sauces on the table and watched as Mojo bounced toward the second door that led through to the pantry and then into the kitchen.

The original Victorian had been designed with a flow that lent itself to regularly serving big meals. When it had been built in the late 1800's, out here on the remote point of the bay, there'd been little else nearby. So the pantry was generous and meant to stock a goodly amount of supplies. It only made sense that it was connected both to the dining room and the kitchen, the three rooms together that were devoted to food.

"Oh, I see," she said, following the pudgy black cat. "Is it snack time?"

But rather than go to the kitchen, he took a sharp turn and angled off into the pantry. Maris frowned as she followed him. His smoked salmon was in the refrigerator, as he well knew. What could he want in the pantry?

Like the kitchen, the storage room had been completely updated. The architecture remained the same, with its curved ceiling coves and the decorative plaster medallions overhead, but the rolling shelves were shallow enough to view all of the essentials. The drawers at their bottoms were done in clear plexiglass, revealing all the contents, and the spice cabinets folded out from the walls to minimize the waste of space. At the far end was a short metal refrigerator used only for wine.

As Maris watched, Mojo jumped up to one of the shelves. On it were Cookie's baking supplies.

"Careful now," she warned him. "You don't want to mess with that stuff."

But of course he ignored her, reaching out a paw. As Maris rushed over to him, it looked as though he'd been reaching for the plastic container of confectioner's sugar. But now it seemed he wanted the pastry flour next to it. Finally though, when she could see past him, his paw was wedged between the two.

"What are you doing?" she muttered, gently picking him up. "What's in there?"

As she drew him into her arms, his paw came out from the darkness, its claws dragging something with it. For a moment she dreaded seeing some type of dead rodent, but when it finally emerged it was a...tarot deck.

"What?" she said, gingerly disengaging his claws from it. "Why is this in here?"

Normally the tarot deck would be in the parlor, along with the Ouija board. Both were available to guests for their enjoyment or entertainment, although Mojo seemed to get more use out of them than anyone.

But as she looked at the box of cards, she realized it was open and one was sticking out. Mojo tried to paw it, so she held it at arm's length, then set it on the shelf. With the tips of her fingers, she removed the protruding card.

"The Magician," she said, laying it down. As Mojo purred, she tapped her temple, calling up the little booklet of tarot interpretation in her photographic memory.

The Magician stood with an arm stretched upward toward the universe, while the other pointed down to the earth. There was a table in front of him and on it were the four symbols of the tarot suits: a cup, a wand, a pentacle, and a sword. They each symbolized an element: water, fire, earth, and air. Above his head was the infinity symbol and around his waist was a snake that was biting its own tail, both symbolizing unlimited potential. In the foreground were flowers and greenery meant to show his aspirations coming to fruition.

Maris was immediately drawn to the cup. It looked like a wine goblet, which made sense. The wand, if you squinted, looked more like a club.

Was Mojo trying to tell her about the blunt force trauma in the wine cellar?

Or was he trying to say that one of the magic folk of Pixie Point Bay was responsible?

But before she could question him, there was a knock at the front door. She checked through the pantry's window toward the front of the house and saw a car that she didn't recognize.

Who would be knocking?

She packed up the tarot cards and put Mojo down.

"Thank you, Mojo," she said to him. As he sat and began to lick his paw, she headed back to the hallway.

13

Friedrich Krone stood on the front porch holding a small wooden box in front of him.

"Mr. Krone," Maris said, as she opened the door. "What a pleasant surprise. Please come in."

"Thank you," he said, in a pleasant baritone. As Maris stood aside it occurred to her that she'd never heard him speak in a normal tone of voice. His faint German accent was even stronger when he wasn't shouting.

"Is Charlie Gorian here?" the vintner asked, looking around.

As Maris closed the door, she said, "Although Charlie is a guest here, I'm afraid he's not here at the moment." She motioned him through to the living room. "Would you like to put that down and have a seat?"

Although she suspected from the frown on Friedrich's face that he wanted nothing more than to simply drop the box and leave, he managed to muster some old-world politeness.

"Yes," he said, wearing a forced smile. "That would be...nice."

She indicated the ottoman. "You can set the box there if you'd like."

"Thank you," he said. The tall man lowered it and gently put it down. Maris could see that the Crown symbol of the winery had been burned into the small wood planks of its top. "A couple of magnums."

"How nice," she said, smiling. "No doubt Charlie will be pleased."

"Well," the vintner said, sounding as though that might be true, "it's the least I could do."

Maris recalled what Charlie had said about the 1947 St-Emilion.

"I'm going to get some tea," she said. "Can I get you a coffee or tea perhaps? Or a glass of water?"

He actually seemed to consider it. "Tea would be nice," he said.

"Good," Maris said. "I'll be right back."

In the kitchen, she selected one of Cookie's special mixes for the winemaker, something particularly relaxing. For herself, she picked something more invigorating. As they steeped, she put some of the homemade sugar cookies on a small plate. To the tray she added some lemon slices, sugar, and napkins. Then she took them all to the living room.

Friedrich sat in one of the high back chairs, but had taken a small statue of a lighthouse from the nearby built-in bookcase.

"You know," he said, setting it back in its place with his long reach, "I knew your aunt."

Maris paused. "No, I didn't know that." She put the serving tray on the coffee table, picked up his tea, and handed it to him. "Lemon and sugar are here," she said, pointing to the tray. "And these are some of our own sugar cookies. Excellent with the tea." She took a seat on the couch. "How did you know her?"

He took a sip of the tea and nodded a little. "This is very good," he said, before setting the china cup back down in its saucer. "She was a frequent customer," he said. "She made purchases for this B&B."

Though his voice hadn't carried a hint of recrimination, she felt it nonetheless. In the months since she'd been running the B&B, she hadn't made a single purchase from his winery.

"That's interesting that you say that," she said, after sipping her tea. "We still have a supply of Crown Winery wine. I'm glad to know it's a holdover from Aunt Glenda's time." She picked up the plate of cookies, pale yellow circles topped with a dusting of confetti colored sprinkles, and offered it to him.

He took one and looked around the room, then out the window to the ocean. "As often as I saw Glenda," he said, "I've never been here. It's beautiful." He took a bite of the cookie. "Oh, that's good." Then he sipped his tea again.

As Maris watched, the vintner relaxed back into his chair and his expression even softened.

"How long have you been making wine, Mr. Krone?" she asked.

"All my life really," he said. "First in Saxony, then in Provence, and finally here. I am a fifth generation vintner."

"Five generations," she said, impressed. "Wine must run in your veins."

He laughed a little, and Maris glimpsed some of the charm that seemed to suffuse his son. "You could say that, I think."

"Did you learn from your father?"

Friedrich nodded after taking another sip of tea. "He was a tough man, very exacting, but when he praised you, it was real. He didn't coddle his family, his employees, or his grapes." He smiled a little at that. "He always said that both people and grapes needed some stress to be as good as they could be."

Maris had to laugh a little. "I guess it worked, seeing as how you run your own winery." She paused to sip her tea. "So that would make your son the sixth generation."

His expression suddenly clouded and, despite the effects of the tea, his jaw clenched. "Him," he spat.

"I happened to be at the winery this morning," she said calmly. "In the crushing room."

"Oh were you?" he said, putting his saucer and cup on the coffee table, along with the unfinished cookie. "Along with everyone else it seems."

"Harlan?" she asked.

The vintner's hands came together in a tangle, his knuckles turning white. "I still can't believe it. In the middle of our own harvest, volunteering at theirs. Of all places, *theirs*." He shook his head and glared at the box of wine. "I've been over this already, with that policeman." He showed her the pads of his fingers. Each was stained a faint black. "I was even fingerprinted." He rubbed his hands together. "It's hard to get off." Again he shook his head, but this time he stood. "Well, small as my harvest may be, I'd better get back to it." As Maris stood, he nodded to her. "Thank you for your hospitality."

"It's my pleasure, Mr. Krone," she said pleasantly.

"May I leave the wine?" he asked, glaring at it again.

"Of course," she said. "I'll let Charlie know you've brought it for him." As she escorted him to the front door, she thought of asking him about seeing Charlie with Dom Alegra before he was murdered. But rather than risk another angry outburst, she asked about something else that puzzled her. "Is your harvest typically small, or is it perhaps the weather this year?"

Just as he opened the front door, he stopped. "This year?" he demanded. "Every year. Every year it gets smaller, ever since Alegra Winery opened." He held up a hand to her as if to stop her response, though she didn't have any. "Oh, yes, I've heard all the theories about soil depletion and changing weather. But it started the day that Alegra broke ground." His tightly closed, pursed lips moved as though he were chewing something. Suddenly, he erupted, as though he couldn't stop. "They're stealing my water! How do you grow grapes without water?"

Maris's eyebrows arched. "Stealing your water? I don't understand how–"

"From the water table," he said, managing not to shout. "The underground water that runs under both our properties."

"But if it's–"

He waved her off. "I've been over this a million times already. No one wants to listen." He gave her a curt nod. "Thank you again."

With that he stomped down the front

porch steps and went to his large work van. Although Maris closed the door, she stood for a moment as the Crown Winery van pulled back.

Why would a fifth generation vintner, who'd made wine in Germany, France, and here, be convinced that he was losing water if he actually wasn't? As she went back to the living room, she gazed down at the small crate of wine. And was he bringing wine to Charlie in thanks for the rare bottle, or was he making an overture, now that Dominic was dead?

As the afternoon wound on, Maris pondered these questions as she did some light housekeeping—straightening up the public rooms and emptying the trash. Bear was kind enough to take the magnums up to Charlie's room before leaving for the day. Cookie retired early to her room and Charlie had yet to return.

As the sun began to dip toward the purple line of the horizon, Maris reviewed the guest calendar. Although two couples were arriving today, it was going to be a late arrival—too late for the Wine Down. Though it didn't happen often, Maris decided she wouldn't be serving wine and cheese today.

"Just as well," she muttered.

It'd been a long and too eventful day. She went to the library and took down a book at random. It'd be another couple of hours before the new guests arrived. After she turned on the Tiffany lamp and took a seat, she took a look at what she'd selected and opened it.

"Trilby," she read from the title page. "By George du Maurier. 1899." She felt the brush of warm fur against her ankle, and looked down at the floor. "Mojo." She patted her lap. "Come on up." He lightly jumped up, did a single turn, and settled down into a fluffy ball, tucking his front paws underneath him. She showed him the book. "Have you read this one?" When he didn't answer, she said, "Me either." She turned to the first page. "It was a fine, sunny, showery day in April," she read, and Mojo purred.

14

In the morning, as they did every day, Maris and Mojo left the bedroom and followed the wonderful aroma of breakfast the short distance to the kitchen. From the giant stove at the far end, Cookie looked over her shoulder and smiled. "Good morning, you two. Sleep well?"

"Like a log," Maris said. "Both of us." As though to echo her, Mojo gave his signature meow, making both Cookie and Maris laugh. "Couldn't have said it better, Mojo."

"I swear that cat of yours understands us," Cookie said, as Maris came to the stove to see what smelled so good. "Isn't that right, Mojo?"

But in reply, he went to his bowl, sat down next to it, and started to clean his face.

Maris smiled down at the chef. "Oh, he understands us all right. He's just not letting on. That would be too easy." She eyed the skillet and the thick handmade tortillas standing by. "Breakfast Burritos?"

"Time to change it up a bit," Cookie said, nodding.

She was scrambling together eggs, crispy hash browns, local caught lox, and three local cheeses from Cheeseman Village. The aroma was absolutely intoxicating. "Oh," Maris said. "My favorite."

Cookie regarded her as she put a hand on her hip. "Hold on. I thought 'Breakfast Pie in a Skillet' was your favorite."

Maris grinned at her. "Of course it is—until you make Breakfast Burritos."

"You can't have two favorites," the chef said, her brow furrowing as she turned back to the stove.

"Sure I can," Maris assured her. "It's one of the many talents I possess, particularly with food." She stood back to take in the rest of the kitchen and clasped her hands together, rubbing them. "What can I do to help?"

For a long moment Cookie said nothing,

and Maris had to stifle an impish grin. She knew she was a disaster in the kitchen. They both knew it. There was nothing, even something as simple as cracking an egg, that she couldn't manage to muff. Even so, she couldn't help but take just a tiny bit of a naughty-girl delight in teasing her friend.

"I know," Maris exclaimed, as though she'd just thought of something. "I'll get the warming trays ready."

Cookie's shoulders relaxed a little. "If you think can manage," she said, looking over her shoulder and giving Maris a wink.

Maris narrowed her eyes at the older woman. Who had been teasing who, she wondered.

When Maris moved the first warming tray to the dining room's sideboard, she found that Cookie had already brought out sides of guacamole, pico de gallo, and even Delia's hot sauces. It was the perfect breakfast for guests to try them. As Maris turned on the tray, it occurred to her that the choice of Breakfast Burritos had been by design.

Back in the kitchen, Mojo's orange eyes followed her and he gave a plaintive little meow. Properly washed, he was ready for his breakfast. Maris took his smoked salmon from the refrigerator and put a portion in his dish. Before she could get out of his way, he used the top of his head to nudge her hand aside.

"Um," she said, backing up. "Bon appétit."

"While you're there," Cookie said, when Maris was stowing the salmon, "could you get the blueberry yogurt?"

"Of course," Maris said.

"I think that turquoise-colored glass bowl would work for it." The chef began moving the finished burritos to the metal tray.

"Good idea," Maris said.

With the yogurt complete and beautifully displayed next to the homemade granola at the beginning of the buffet, Cookie placed a bowl of fresh berries just behind it. The two of them stood back for a moment, and nodded simultaneously.

Fresh sourdough bread next to the toaster, along with small cylindrical curls of the ultra creamy butter from the Cheeseman Village dairy, finished off the breakfast buffet, and not a moment too soon.

"Good morning, Maris," Charlie said. "Good morning, Cookie."

Though he smiled pleasantly, the boyish grin had gone and the dark circles under his eyes said he hadn't slept well. The shock of Dominic Alegra's death—or possibly the shock of being a suspect—could easily account for being sleepless. But as usual, he wore a crisply pressed dark blue shirt, matching tie, and a nicely tailored business suit.

"Good morning, Charlie," Maris said. "There's freshly squeezed orange juice in the decanter, and just brewed coffee in the carafe."

He picked up one of the china cups and a saucer. "I think I'll just start with some coffee."

"Did you get the wine magnums that Mr. Krone brought by?" she asked, as she picked up a plate and Cookie began to make some tea.

"Oh, is that how that got there?" he said and smiled. "I should have guessed." He looked at her. "Yes, I did get those. Thank you."

A young couple appeared in the doorway. "Good morning," the woman said. Kate Palmer and her husband George looked to be in their early to mid thirties. A petite, dark-eyed brunette, she contrasted with her tall, lanky, and already graying husband.

"Good morning, Kate, George," Maris said. They'd arrived with another couple last night, all of them traveling together. "Cookie's to-die-for Breakfast Burritos are in the warming trays, and we've also got homemade granola with blueberry yogurt which is made locally."

George's eyes lit up as he surveyed the buffet. "It looks wonderful." He picked up a plate and served himself a burrito, followed by Kate, who did the same.

Not five seconds later, their friends arrived. "I see we're not the only early risers," Sarah Kelton said smiling. "Good morning, everybody.

Her husband William followed her. "I'm on vacation," he said. "There's no such thing as early rising."

Like their friends, the second couple were the same age and just as upbeat. While William was dark complected with an artful stubble of beard, his wife was fair-haired and green-eyed. Also like the other couple, something about their perfectly coiffed hair, upscale fashion sense, and expensive jewelry spoke to them all being affluent.

Maris took her plate to the long table, making sure not to sit with Cookie. Eating with the guests was a tradition at the B&B, one to which Maris had easily warmed. It encouraged conversation, and she enjoyed hearing about the lives and jobs of their visitors.

For a few minutes, the foursome explained that the two men were financial analysts and the two women were real estate agents. The women had known each other first, and then found that their husbands knew each other as well.

"Talk about a small world," Sarah said, smiling.

"Are you planning on seeing any of the local sights?" Cookie asked. To Maris's surprise she was sprinkling some of Delia's hot sauce onto her plate.

"If that includes the wineries down south," William said, "then yes."

"We're here for the wine harvest," his wife Sarah said.

"All the way from Canada," Kate added.

"But we've always heard so many great things about it."

At the talk of wine, Charlie perked up. "You heard right," he said. "You're going to visit one of the best wineries at the best time of year. Bar none."

Maris nodded to him. "Charlie Gorian, may I introduce Sarah, Kate, George, and William. They joined us last night. Everyone, Charlie Gorian." There were murmurs of acknowledgement all around.

"So, Charlie," George said, sprinkling some hot sauce on his pico de gallo. "You've already been to the wineries here?"

"Many times," he said, his boyish smile back. "I'm a repeat offender."

"And not just here," Maris prompted.

"Oh?" said Sarah, her pencil thin eyebrow raised. "We travel for wine too. Maybe we've visited some of the same wineries."

But by the time Charlie finished rattling off the extensive list of worldwide wine regions he'd visited, the four other guests stared at him in stunned silence. As though talking of wine had improved his appetite, Charlie finally went to the sideboard and took a burrito.

He lifted the plate to his nose. "This smells amazing."

Cookie nodded to him. "Thank you."

"Are you saying you've tasted wine at….all of those locations?" William asked.

Charlie decided to stand and eat. As he chopped into the burrito with the side of his fork, he shrugged. "That's my job."

"Your job," Kate said, envy in her voice. She glanced at her companions. "Nice work if you can get it."

Charlie grinned at her. "You won't hear me complaining." Then he took a bite of the burrito and made an appreciative sound. He nodded his head, swallowing. "Wonderful." He looked at the four other guests. "You hear a lot about the charm and hospitality of the Bordeaux region, or Champagne, but believe me when I tell you that the Lighthouse and B&B of Pixie Point Bay outshines them all."

Maris grinned and lifted her orange juice to him. "Thank you, Charlie."

"Anything local you care to recommend, Charlie?" George asked. "You know, in terms of wine or tasting."

Although the young man took a breath and seemed about to launch into an answer, he paused. Then he eyed the other guests. "I'll tell you what. Rather than have me tell you, I can show you." He looked at Maris. "Perhaps this evening? I could maybe host a little tasting?"

"Really?" Sarah crowed. "That'd be *amazing*."

"With our host's permission, of course," Charlie said, inclining his head to Maris.

"I think that would be delightful," Maris said. "We usually begin our Wine Down around sunset."

"Wine Down," Charlie muttered and laughed a little. "I'm going to have to steal that one from you." He chopped into his burrito again. "Sunset it is, if everyone is game?"

"Absolutely," Sarah said, reinforced by yeses from the others.

For a few moments, they ate in silence.

"I must say," Cookie said to Maris. "These hot sauces from Delia's are really wonderful."

Maris nodded. "I have to agree—in moderation."

"This one is wonderful," George said, picking up the bottle. "Delia's Sizzling Smokehouse of Pixie Point Bay. I might have to get some before we leave." He eyed Charlie's plate. "You not a spice fan, Charlie?"

The young wine investor shook his head, as he finished his burrito. Then he quickly wiped his mouth with a napkin. "I'm tasting later today. I want to keep my palate neutral."

For an awkward moment, the other four guests stared down at their plates.

Finally, Kate said, "Oh."

"But let me give you a tip before you go," Charlie said. "Something only the pros really do." Almost as one, the two couples leaned toward him. "No cologne or perfume."

"What?" William said. "But..."

Charlie shook his head. "Smell is a huge part of taste. Don't bias your palate with a pre-existing aroma, no matter how much you like it."

William's wife Sarah stood up. "Dibs on the shower," she said, making everyone laugh.

Charlie returned his empty plate to the tray on the sideboard before turning to Cookie. "Thank you for the lovely breakfast." Then he turned to the rest of the group. "I'll see you at sunset."

15

As Cookie rinsed, Maris loaded the dishwasher.

"Another smash hit buffet," Maris told the chef. "And that was nice of you to put out Delia's hot sauces."

"I think they were a nice compliment," Cookie said. "And that was very generous of Charlie." She passed Maris a plate. "The other guests seemed very excited about some tasting tips."

Maris slotted the plate into a spot next to some others. "It was," she agreed, but couldn't help but frown. "I think it's going to be...fun."

Cookie eyed her. "You say 'fun' like you're going to have a front row seat at a medieval inquisition for witches."

Maris grimaced a bit. "No, I think it'll be fun for the guests."

The diminutive chef handed her the forks. "But not for you."

"It's not that it won't be fun," Maris said quickly, but stopped herself. She loaded the utensils and put her damp hands on her hips. "You know what it is?" Cookie was about to hand her a serving spoon but paused. "It's the fact that he's a wine expert—and I'm not."

Cookie waved the serving spoon as though she could move aside Maris's doubt. "Tosh. It's just for an evening. Let him be the expert. You're the *host*, and a very good one at that." She gestured around the kitchen. "This isn't a winery, and people don't stay here for wine tastings. They're here for hospitality." She handed Maris the serving spoon. "They're here for comfort and relaxation. Giving *that* to them is our job."

As Maris resumed loading the dishwasher, they were both quiet for some time. She thought of the many hundreds of Wine Downs she'd hosted over the decades. She'd never studied wine, just followed her instincts. But having an expert look over your shoulder...

"You've never seen my red velvet crepes," Cookie said.

Maris blinked at her. "I'm sorry. Your what?" She took the rinsed bowl that the chef offered to her.

"My red velvet crepes filled with strawberries, sour cream, cardamon, and ginger."

"Wow," Maris said, holding the bowl. "No, I think I'd remember."

Cookie nodded. "I think you would. But there's a reason I don't make them any more."

They sounded amazing, and probably looked it too. "Why not?" Maris loaded the bowl, filling the dishwasher to capacity.

"Because I made them to impress people, to show off. Do you know that there's a theme my buffets follow now?"

Maris thought back, not only on this morning's offerings, but the various breakfasts over the last number of months. For the life of her, though, she couldn't see a common denominator.

"Comfort food," Cookie said, drying off her hands. "Good ingredients, made well. Nothing flashy. Just tasty and filling. Because it's not about me. It's about our guests."

Maris smiled at the older woman. It had

never occurred to her that Cookie would, of course, be capable of all kinds of meals. There were certainly hints of it in the buffet from time to time. But the food was mostly on the simple side, and what people away from home might appreciate to start their day.

Cookie put the dishwasher soap in the dispenser and closed the door. "It's the same with the evening meal," she said, pushing the start button. "Because that's what the Wine Down really is—enough for a meal. How do you pick the food?"

Maris spread her hands. "I pair it with a couple of wines, and try not to overwhelm the cheeseboard with too much variety. That never works. All it does is confuse the tastebuds."

Cookie grinned at her. "Exactly. You could throw a million things at them. Impress them with all sorts of rare wines or pungent cheeses. You must have come across a few."

Maris nodded. "At this point? Yeah, I imagine there's very little I haven't seen."

Cookie regarded her for a few moments. "Right. So tonight?"

Maris smiled. "It's about the guests, as always. All of them, including the wine investor." She put a hand on Cookie's shoulder. "And it'll be fun. It really will be."

Cookie winked at her. "Glad to hear it."

By the time they were done with the cleanup, everyone had left. But rather than begin tidying the rooms, Maris was curious. She was no wine expert, nor did she need to be, but it never hurt to learn a little. The tour of the winery, the fact that Charlie intended to buy the entire release, and that people invested in wine for a living were all new to her.

Back in her room, she booted up her little used laptop. As she searched for wine investing, an entire world of wine auctions and catalogs opened up. One click led to another until she was visiting auction houses in New York and London, or wineries in Australia and Napa, and gala events in Beijing. It looked like you could actually get a degree in wine making, and there were even world championships for sommeliers.

"Amazing," she muttered.

She was just about to power down the computer, when another intriguing thought occurred to her. She searched for the 1947 St-Emilion. It came up immediately, mostly at auction sites. The Chateau Cheval Blanc 1947 St-Emilion was the Bordeaux wine against which all others were measured. Ironically, the great postwar wine had almost not come into being. During a bout of hellishly hot weather, the fermentation had 'stuck.' But the vintner stood in line daily in order to buy blocks of ice to get it going again. Though it hadn't been his intention, he'd created one of the most memorable and sought-after wines in the world. To his credit, he'd never tried to claim it was anything more than what it was —a deliriously happy accident.

Maris looked at various images of the rare wine. "History in a bottle," she said.

Again, one click led to another as she dove down the rabbit hole of French wines, only to emerge an hour later. Head swimming, she finally closed the computer. That was enough for one day—actually, more like one month. It was time to get some cleaning done at the B&B.

16

Maris spent the rest of the day playing catch-up with her B&B chores. Cookie had already finished her duties and was out in the garden working solo. As Maris shifted into high gear, she dusted all the furniture downstairs and vacuumed the floors. Occasionally she answered the phone and took reservations as well.

In the middle of the day, the leftover crab sandwich was a lifesaver—and she wolfed it down. Then it was time to do the upstairs. Cookie had already taken care of the bathrooms, making sure fresh towels and ample toiletries were available. Maris saw to turning down the beds of the five guests, and also emptying the trash.

In Charlie's room, she saw the Crown Winery box of magnums that Friedrich had brought. It was on the floor where Bear had left it. She paused for a moment, looking at it, but not because of the upcoming evening's wine and cheese. Instead her thoughts drifted again to yesterday, when she'd seen the young wine investor in the tasting room at Alegra Winery. He'd been excited to be bringing his gift to Dom. Then, according to his interview with Mac, Dominic Alegra had shared it with an angry Friedrich Krone. Assuming that was true, it accounted for three glasses, not four.

Who else had been there?

She frowned as she took the collected trash downstairs. Neither Charlie nor Friedrich had mentioned seeing someone other than Dom. As she came down the back stairs and into the hallway, she noticed the long, dark shadows inching their way across the floor. The sun was sinking and the entire day seemed as though it'd simply slipped away. She was tired from all the cleaning—thank goodness it didn't have to be done every day—but she hadn't realized how late it'd gotten.

But as she passed the parlor for probably the fiftieth time that day, she had to stop. Mojo was on the Ouija board.

"Finally," she said lowly. "It's about time."

By the time she quietly came to the side of the pudgy little black cat, he'd already taken a seat and gone still. Although his body was amazingly motionless and his glittering orange eyes had taken on the usual thousand-yard stare, his ears cocked in every direction. Like small and fur-lined antennae, they rotated in near circles as he seemed to actually hear something that she couldn't. Maris glanced at the image of the woman on the corner of the board, her hands reaching forward even as a floating head behind her seemed to be saying something into her ear.

Could Mojo actually be hearing the voices of the spirits? It would be like Aunt Glenda to rescue a cat with magical abilities. She crossed her arms and watched him but didn't have to wait long. Without looking down, he placed a paw directly on the planchette.

He started with the letter W.

"W," Maris said quietly. "Wine?"

With a little flick of his leg, he moved the

plastic disc over the nearby "I" in the first row.

"You have got to be kidding me," she whispered.

Then, almost as far as he could reach and remain sitting, he pushed the transparent plastic over the "N" at the left of the board.

Maris put both hands on her hips.

As expected, he finished by moving the planchette over the "E" before stopping. Then he blinked his big eyes and looked up at her.

"Seriously, Mojo?" she said, exasperated. "Wine? Couldn't you narrow it down a little? Wine was everywhere."

In answer, he simply shook out his fur, and jumped lightly to the floor. He looked over at the board and then at her, and gave his tiny, tinny harmonica-like meow. Then he bounced out of the room.

"Wine?" she said again. Of course the murder involved wine. It took place at a winery. Dom had been surrounded by it. He made it. He'd been drinking it. She threw her hands in the air and shook her head. "Wine," she muttered.

As she stepped into the hallway she saw

her fluffy cat disappearing into their bedroom. "Thanks," she called out after him.

But really, thanks for what? His clues were often inscrutable, but this one was downright obvious. She put a hand to her chin as she thought. Perhaps the letters stood for something, like an acronym.

The sound of tires crunching on the gravel at the front of the house's long driveway drew her attention that way. Charlie's red Bentley had just pulled up.

Through the front door's leaded window, Maris could see Charlie carrying a large cardboard box that looked full—not only of wines but also groceries. She hurried forward and opened the door just before he got there.

"Great timing," he said, grinning at her.

"Goodness," she said. "What's all this?" She closed the door behind him.

He headed down the hall. "Well, if you don't mind, I'd like to skip the cheeseboard and use my go-to palate cleansers." He ducked into the kitchen and put the box on the big butcher block. "If that'd be okay with you, of course."

Maris spread her hands. "Absolutely. I don't mind at all." She peeked into the box.

Tucked among the bottles of wine were bags of pita chips, a couple of pineapples, and celery. She was already learning something. "Interesting." She stood back. "What can I do to help?"

"Not a thing," he said, doffing his jacket and tossing it over one of the stools. "But please have a seat." Although the hostess in her wanted to jump in and do something, her feet and back ached from the hectic cleaning day. When she hesitated, he added, "Please, I insist. This is actually a fun part for me."

In her head, Maris heard Cookie's voice telling her to slow down and she almost had to smile to herself. The chef's constant reminders to stop her Type A+ personality behavior in order to save herself from the type of heart attack that had killed both her aunt and mother must have sunk in—at least a little.

She pulled out one of the stools. "I'd be delighted to watch someone else do all the work." As she took a seat, she exhaled a little. It felt good to sit.

Charlie turned toward the many cabinets. "Where are the platters and big bowls?" he asked.

"The door at the end, on the second shelf."

He went and opened that cabinet. "Perfect," he said, lifting the top one. But as he tilted the large glass platter toward him, a small tinkling bell sounded, followed by a skittering sound. A little, lattice work, purple and yellow plastic ball rolled off, flew past his head, over his shoulder, and landed on the tile floor.

"Oh no," Maris muttered. Its little bell jingled merrily as it rolled to her feet. But rather than pick it up, she jumped up and went to Charlie. "Here," she said, taking the platter from him. "Let me wash this."

It was Charlie who went to the butcher block and crouched to pick up the ball, making it tinkle again. "What's this?" he said.

A tiny, tinny meow answered him. As though summoned by the sound of his toy, Mojo bounced quickly into the room and trotted over to Charlie.

Maris inwardly cringed. How Mojo got his toys into such places she didn't know. But it seemed there was nowhere, not even in their kitchen, where he couldn't hide them. He had to have the largest stash of toys of any cat in the western hemisphere, and yet she'd never stumbled across it. She quickly rinsed water over the platter and soaped the sponge.

"Who is this?" Charlie said, still crouching.

Maris half-turned from the sink. "That would be Mojo, and you've found one of his toys." One of his *many* toys, she added mentally.

"Isn't he a beauty," Charlie said, giving him the ball and stroking his back. Mojo immediately dropped the ball and purred. "And friendly." He stroked his back again. "Hi there, Mojo."

By the time Maris was done washing and drying the platter, Mojo had clearly made another conquest. She took a bowl from the cabinet as well. Once it was clean she set it on the butcher block next to the platter. "Here you go."

With a final scratch behind the ears, he stood. "Thanks," he said, as he went to the sink and washed his hands. Then he fetched the celery and pineapples.

"Have you been working here all day?" he asked. "I'll bet owning a B&B is a lot of work."

As she took her seat at the butcher block

again, she rested her elbows on it. "It comes and goes. Sometimes it can get a bit hectic, other times it's pretty quiet."

"Does it change with the seasons?"

Maris thought about it for a moment. "You now, I'm not sure. I haven't been here all that long, and the seasons don't particularly change a lot."

"Ah," Charlie said, smiling, as he carefully cleaned the celery. "The beauty of the Middle Kingdom. It's always a pleasant day here."

Maris laughed a little. "Exactly," she said. "How long have you been visiting?"

He smirked a little as he began to rinse the pineapple. "Since Dominic started winning medals." He paused, his expression sobering, and he looked down into the sink. "What an amazing vintner he was."

Maris recalled what Eugene had said. "Well, we can always hope that Rosamel decides to carry on with the family tradition."

Charlie gave her a little smile. "That's right." He nodded. "There's always hope." He brought the celery and pineapple to the butcher block and began slicing them.

Maris glanced at the floor and saw that Mojo was watching as well. Perhaps it intrigued her little cat to see someone other than Cookie or herself cooking or prepping. But as Maris returned her attention to Charlie, watching him artfully arranging the strange little assortment of food, she found herself relaxing. The tension began to drain from her shoulders and neck. It was strangely satisfying to see someone else getting together the ingredients for the Wine Down, and his touch was sure and deft.

"I'd guess this isn't your first time," Maris said, elbow on butcher block and resting her chin in her hand.

Charlie shook his head as he smiled. "I grew up in the kitchen. Everything I know, my mom taught me."

"Was she a cook?"

"I think nowadays she'd be called a domestic technician," he said, arranging the pineapple on the platter. "She was at home full-time. My brother and I were a bit of a handful."

"Really," Maris said, looking at the perfectly groomed young man. "That's hard to imagine."

He smirked as he eyed the platter. "Well, maybe my brother more than me." He opened a bag of pita chips, and poured some out. "But all credit to her. She raised two boys who finished college."

It sounded to Maris as though the father hadn't been in the picture. She knew what that was like. Her own father had died in a car accident when she was away at school.

Charlie stood back and regarded the food: celery pieces to one side, pineapple sections to the other, and pita chips in the middle. "That'll do it."

Maris stood and indicated the platter. "To the dining room?"

Charlie nodded. "If you don't mind." He put the large bowl in the box with the wines and picked it up. "I'll bring these."

The sound of the front door opening caught Maris's attention. As she and Charlie exited into the hallway, both the Palmers and Keltons arrived home. The foursome had been talking and laughing, but Sarah's eyes immediately went to the box of bottles.

Maris grinned at them. "Great timing."

18

———

As Maris set down the tray on the dining table, Charlie unpacked the box at the sideboard, and the two couples followed them in.

"I've been looking forward to this all day," Sarah said.

"I can't believe we get to taste wines here at home," George agreed.

Maris smiled at them as Charlie retrieved a corkscrew from his pocket and opened it. It always gave her a sense of satisfaction when guests referred to the B&B as 'home.'

"While I'm uncorking the wines," Charlie told everyone, "please have a piece of celery. It will cleanse the palate. We'll all start with a blank slate, so to speak."

Everyone dutifully took a piece and began munching.

"I adore celery anyway," Kate said.

For a few moments, everyone simply chewed and watched Charlie opening bottles. Maris noted that he always placed the labels facing the wall or himself when he handled them. It appeared as though it was going to be a blind tasting. When he pulled the last cork free, he said, "There's only one rule when it comes to wine tasting." He paused for a dramatic moment, taking a piece of celery. "Enjoy yourself."

That brought smiles all around.

"I wouldn't call myself a rule-follower," William said, "but I think I can live with that."

"Good," Charlie said. "Everything we're going to do here tonight has just that one aim: to make your wine tastings more enjoyable."

"How many wines do you think you've tasted, Charlie?" George asked.

The young investor paused for a moment, still eating his celery. His eyes went to the floor and he actually seemed to be counting. "Including today..." He started to count on his fingers and then broke off in a laugh. "Honestly, thousands."

"Thousands," muttered Sarah, with awe in her voice.

Charlie took the bowl from the box and put it on the table next to the platter.

"How do you remember them all?" William asked.

Charlie took out his phone. "I don't, but I take comprehensive notes. Which reminds me. Everyone take out your phones. Use whatever app you like to record your thoughts. We're going to start with the whites." He brought forward the white wine glasses, selected one of the bottles and poured a little into each. "If there's a wine you don't like, just pour it in the bowl." He handed a glass to Sarah, and then Kate. "Also, don't feel obliged to taste everything. It's completely up to you." As he finished distributing the glasses, he added, "And it's great to take pictures too—of the glass or the bottle, although I won't be showing that to you right away. Whatever you think might help you later, do it."

"Oh, wow," George muttered. "I never thought about taking pictures."

Charlie lifted the wine in his glass to the overhead light fixture as the beams from the setting sun began to fade. "Tasting is about much more than taste. We're going to use all the senses, starting with vision." He tilted his glass. "Coat the sides of the glass with the wine and look at the legs—the drips as they fall down. The thicker the legs, the more alcohol." He looked at them. "Take a look and then make a note."

They all did, including Maris. She'd heard of legs, of course, but had never realized that they had anything to do with the amount of alcohol. She made a note and estimated their thickness. George also took a picture. When everyone was ready, Charlie continued.

"Next comes smell which, as I mentioned this morning, is supremely important," he said.

"I washed off my Chanel No. 5," Sarah said.

"Good for you," Charlie replied, "and I'll tell you why. Because our sense of smell is far more accurate than our sense of taste." He swirled the wine in his glass. "You want to aerate it a bit." Then he set his glass on the table. "If you're afraid of spilling it, then place it on a flat surface, and move the glass in fast circles while holding it against the table top." He demonstrated. Everyone moved to the table and imitated him. "Now," he said, lifting the glass to his nose. "Inhale deeply." He actually stuck his nose into the glass and took a long, deep sniff. "You can make a note, of course," he said, with his nose still protruding below the rim. "But also try to remember what you smell."

Maris smelled something citrusy, almost like a grapefruit, that made her nose crinkle. She made a note. Charlie smiled and waited patiently as everyone else did the same.

"And now we taste." He held up a finger. "But when you do, pay attention to texture first. How does it make your lips and tongue feel? If they feel dry, that's the tannins. If you pucker, that's acidity."

He took a sip, and held it in his mouth. Everyone followed suit. As Maris took a small taste, she tried to concentrate on her lips and tongue. She was definitely puckering. The wine was on the acidic side. Mouths closed, they all looked at one another, and then at Charlie, who swallowed. As though they'd been waiting for permission, everyone else followed suit. William made a yummy sound.

"After you swallow," Charlie said, "how long does the experience of the wine linger in your mouth? Is it gone already, or can you still taste it. That's the finish: sometimes short, sometimes long, or just average. Go ahead and make your notes."

Though Maris wasn't really sure what to write, it seemed to her that the finish had ended almost immediately. When everyone looked up from their phones, Charlie nodded.

"One final tip," he said. "Remember how it smelled?" He looked around the group, and Maris recalled the grapefruit aroma, nodding. "Did that very first impression of the smell match the taste?"

Maris thought back. In fact it did. The two went together nicely. She made her note.

"Good," Charlie said, when everyone was finished. He gave them all an impish smile. "Any guesses as to the varietal?"

"Sauvignon Blanc," Sarah said immediately.

He inclined his head toward her, and turned the bottle on the side board. It was a

Sauvignon Blanc from Alegra Winery. There were murmurs and smiles all around, and Kate clinked her glass to Sarah's. "Well done, you."

Charlie indicated the platter and bowl. "You can finish your wine if you like, but please have something to eat. Any of these will help to get our palates ready for the next wine."

Although no one emptied their wine, everyone reached to the platter, including Charlie. Maris took a pita chip this time.

"Man, is this fun," William said. "I thought it was going to be like a class or something."

"I just thought we were going to drink wine," George agreed.

Charlie smiled at him. "There is nothing wrong with that, my friend." He nodded to the sideboard and waiting wines. "Shall we proceed to the next?"

A few hearty yeses answered him.

As he led them through the same steps for the other wines, Maris was astonished at how different they all tasted. Perhaps he'd chosen them for that reason, or perhaps using all the senses made that much of a difference, but she couldn't remember ever feeling so capable of distinguishing between the various whites and reds. In the end, the wines had come from both Alegra and Crown wineries, and the Alegra wines had proved to be everyone's favorites.

"What's that bottle over there?" Kate asked. "That dusty one behind the rest."

Charlie finished draining his glass of the last red he'd served. "Something rather special. The pièce de résistance." This time there was no hiding of the label or even being coy. He presented it to them as though it was his newborn son. "A 1971 Bordeaux from Domaine Ponsot, the Clos St. Denis Grand Cru. One of my favorites." He gestured to them with the bottle. "And I'd be delighted if you'd share it with me."

"But..." Sarah said, her eyes glued to it. "But that has to be worth..."

Charlie shrugged. "A few thousand dollars." George sputtered and Kate gasped, while William clutched his wine glass to his heart. The wine investor smiled at them. "But what's a few thousand between friends." In the stunned silence that followed, he opened the bottle. Maris exchanged a surprised look with her guests, as Charlie poured the first glass and gave it to Sarah. She set aside the previous glass, holding up the Bordeaux to the light. "There's bound to be a bit of sediment." He poured another and moved on to Kate. "Just ignore it." Then he poured for Maris. "It's not harmful." Once everyone's glasses were full, he lifted his to the group. "To wine tasting in Pixie Point Bay."

They all lifted their glasses. "To wine tasting in Pixie Point Bay."

As Maris took a deep sniff and then a sip, she was immediately struck with the intensity of the flavor, but it had almost no acidity. It was rich and smooth and for a long moment she only held it in her mouth, as the lush flavors of blackberries and black currants washed over her tongue. When she finally swallowed, the finish was long and almost sweet. Not only was it incredible, it was completely unlike any of the other reds they'd had tonight.

"Amazing," Sarah whispered. Her wide eyes stared down into the glass, and then at her husband. "I can't believe this."

He mouthed a silent 'wow.'

"I'm glad we had an early dinner," Kate

said. "Because I'm not eating or drinking any-thing ever again."

There was light laughter from the entire room, including from Charlie.

"Thank you," Maris said, lifting her glass to him. "For this, and for a wonderful evening."

"To Charlie," Sarah said, quickly echoed by the others.

By the time they reluctantly finished their wine, there were hugs all around. As far as the Wine Down was concerned, Charlie had set a new high bar. With the evening ended, the couples bid him and Maris a goodnight before heading upstairs. As she started the cleanup, he helped her take everything to the kitchen.

"Charlie, if you don't mind me asking," Maris said. "How did you get your start in wine?"

He smiled. "An evening not unlike this, actually. Just a casual tasting with friends. It was when I had my first Bordeaux that I jumped in with both feet. I got into wines just as the supply couldn't keep up with the de-mand." Maris loaded the glasses into the dishwasher as he handed them to her. "The prices just got higher and higher, so I invested, sold, and invested more."

"The wine that you brought to Dom," she said, shutting the washer. "That was a Bordeaux as well."

He nodded as he scraped the leftover food into the trash. "That's an excellent example. One of the best. I hope Harlan got a chance to taste it."

Maris paused as she put the empty bottle in the recycle bin. "Harlan? Do you mean Friedrich at Crown Winery?"

"No," he said, putting the platter in the sink. He turned on the water. "I mean Harlan, at Alegra, with Dom and I." He began washing the platter. "He was there having a glass of wine with Dom when I arrived." He turned off the water and toweled off his hands, smiling at her. "I had met him previously, of course, and their business must have been concluded since he left as soon as I arrived."

That would explain the fourth glass, Maris thought. She paused and regarded Charlie.

Had the wine this evening helped to jog his memory? Why hadn't he mentioned Harlan when Mac had interviewed him? Or had it just skipped his mind after the shock of learning of Dom's death?

"I think I'm going to turn in as well," he turned to the kitchen door but paused. "Thanks for lending me your dining room tonight. It's always fun for me to introduce people to my world. Who knows, maybe a vintner was born tonight."

"Or an investor," Maris agreed. "And it was entirely my pleasure. Thank you, again."

With that, he headed to the stairs and then up.

Maris, however, exited to the back porch and then through the garden and into Cookie's greenhouse. She took out her phone and dialed Mac.

19

Though she had to grit her teeth, Maris left the early morning light behind and made her way to Cellar 14 of Alegra Winery. The corridor leading down seemed shorter today, but no brighter. The only truly redeeming aspect of this morning's visit was the person that she was meeting. When she entered the cellar, he was waiting.

"Good morning, Mac," she said, not having to force her smile.

"Good morning, Maris," he said. "Thanks for your call last night." He had been looking through a manila file folder of documents but set it on a barrel head. "Harlan should be here any moment."

"Great," Maris said, and thought, *The sooner, the better.*

As she approached him, she couldn't help but look at the floor where Dom had lain, and also the stain of red wine.

"I'll keep this short," the sheriff said.

He'd seen her staring at where the body had been and probably assumed she was uncomfortable being in the room where the murder had happened. But if that had been true, she could suggest that they simply step outside.

"Sheriff McKenna?" said a man's voice from the door.

Maris turned to see Harlan Krone, almost tall enough that he had to duck through the arched opening. Once again she was struck by the resemblance to his father—except for the full beard and dapper hair cut. Although he was dressed in work clothes, as though he might be volunteering at the Alegra harvest again, they were clean.

"Mr. Krone," Mac said, "please come in."

For a moment, the big man dithered. His eyes glanced around at the shelves of wine bottles, the wooden barrels, the floor and the ceiling. Then he absently stroked his beard before he finally took a step in. The young man looked as anxious as Maris felt. Only then did she realize that must have been Mac's intention, to put Harlan on edge. They could have met anywhere but he'd chosen the murder scene. It actually helped her to relax a little knowing that the cellar was likely a tactic.

"Why didn't you volunteer what you knew about the murder?" Mac asked.

Maris's brows rose just a little. True to his word, he was wasting no time.

Harlan gaped at him. "Because I don't know anything about the murder."

"You were here that morning," Mac said.

"I was just having a glass of wine with Dom," the young man said. "That's all."

"After helping with the harvest here and being dragged away by your father," Maris added.

He regarded her, as though seeing her for the first time. "You were with Rosamel that day."

"Why would you help at the harvest of your competitor?" the sheriff asked.

Harlan's lips pressed into a thin line. "Because they need it."

"Really?" Mac said. "When your own winery is harvesting too?"

Harlan's ice-blue eyes met the sheriff's. "We have enough help."

"So much help," Mac said, "that you have time to have a meeting with your competitor."

"It wasn't a meeting," the young man said stiffly. "It was a glass of wine and I wasn't here long."

"How long were you here?" Mac said, not letting up.

Harlan thought for a moment. "Maybe... ten minutes."

The sheriff gestured to the room. "Where were you standing?" Harlan stroked his beard and pointed to a spot next to one of the barrels. "Show me." The young man slowly moved past Maris and took a position next to the closest barrel. "And where was Mr. Alegra?" Harlan pointed to the other side of the barrel. Mac moved to stand in that place. He looked up at the young man. "Within easy reach."

Harlan swallowed and then frowned. "Look, I don't even know how he died."

"He was struck," Mac said, without offering any further information.

Harlan blinked at him. "Struck?" He glanced at Maris, then looked at Mac. "You mean he was punched?"

Maris watched as Mac processed that information. If Harlan were putting on an act, it was a decent one.

"What was the purpose of your meeting?" the sheriff asked.

Now Harlan scowled and balled his hands into fists. "It wasn't a meeting." His voice was tight and controlled. "There was no purpose. We had wine."

"Oh," Maris said, "speaking of which. Did you get to taste Charlie's 1947 St-Emilion?"

"A 47 St-Emilion?" Harlan said, scowling at her. "The Cheval Blanc? I've never even seen one. Are you saying Charlie Gorian had a bottle of it?"

"He did," Maris replied. "I saw it in the tasting room when he showed it to Rosamel."

"Before he came down here and saw you with Mr. Alegra," Mac said. "What did you discuss while you were having wine? The harvest perhaps?"

Harlan looked as though he was going to shoot back with a retort, but clamped his lips together, taking in a long breath through his nose. "We just had wine."

As anxious as the tall man appeared, he was simply not budging.

"All right, Mr. Krone," Mac said. "I'm not going to bring you in for questioning. But you're not to leave the area. I'll be back in touch with you." He didn't bother with the business card.

"Fine," was all Harlan said, before quickly striding from the room.

As Mac watched him go, he hooked his thumbs behind his utility belt. "'For sparkling was the rosy wine, and private was the chamber.'" He looked at Maris. "Pretty tight-lipped kid."

"Whatever they discussed," Maris said, nodding, "he was obviously very uncomfortable repeating it."

Mac picked up the manila folder from the barrel head. "I've got the forensics results back."

He opened it and was about to show her,

when she said, "Could we look at those out-side?" She'd already stayed longer than she'd anticipated—or wanted. Now that Harlan was gone, there was also no reason to be in the cellar. "It's such lovely weather."

20

Outside at the large circular drive, they sat on one of the visitor benches, under a pretty cedar arbor draped with grape vines. As Mac sat down, he said, "You're right. It really is nice out here."

An older couple passed by, on their way to the winery. A few cars were already parked in the lot. Though the sun was out, she and the sheriff were in the shade, and a soft breeze rustled the grape leaves around them. She was glad to be out of the cellar, but it also happened to be a very pleasant day.

"It really is," she agreed.

Mac opened the manila folder. "The coroner has confirmed what he observed on the scene. Blunt force trauma to the back of the head killed Dominic Alegra." He handed the report to her. "Very likely caused by a wine bottle, given the curvature of the skull fragments."

The various facts on the sheet of paper included a likely radius for the bottle. But other than that figure, they did little to add to what they already knew. She shook her head. "Unfortunately, there must be thousands of bottles in that cellar." She handed back the report.

Mac took it and nodded as he said, "The murder weapon could even have been that expensive gift that Charlie Gorian brought."

She recalled the previous evening, and how the young wine investor had led them through the wine tasting, finishing with the rare Bordeaux. There was something about the old bottle of wine...something that was relevant.

Mac leafed through the other paperwork. "The crime scene investigators also tested the wine that was spattered across the floor."

Though she'd been trying to figure out what was important about the old bottle of wine, she came back to the moment. "Spattered? Do you mean spilled?"

He handed her a photo of the floor. "No. It's spattered. You see the pattern, how it becomes a fine spray at the edge." She did indeed see the roughly oblong pattern of dots. "If it'd been spilled, there'd have been something more like a puddle." He took out another sheet that looked like a chemical analysis. "The spattered wine was mixed with Dominic Alegra's saliva."

"His saliva?" Maris asked. "He had that wine in his mouth?" She tried to imagine the scene. "If he'd been hit in the back of the head while he was drinking, would that do it?"

"It's near where he fell," Mac said. "So it's possible. And of course he had traces of wine in his mouth and stomach, though they haven't identified which wine."

He put the paperwork away. "I'm still waiting on the fingerprints but it seems like we'll have at least Dominic's, Charlie Gorian's, and now both of the Krone's." He glanced back at the winery. "Father and son. Neither of them is telling the truth, or they're hiding something, or both." He closed the folder over. "But fingerprinting every bottle in that cellar isn't going to fly.

It'd be like finding a needle in a needle factory."

Maris suddenly remembered what Charlie had said when they'd been tasting the Bordeaux.

"Hold on," she said. "As far as I know, the wine bottles don't get moved much, if at all. We'd have to check with Rosamel on that. But apparently some sort of sediment settles in older bottles. When you move them around, the sediment moves around too."

Mac narrowed his eyes. "So if one of the bottles down there had been used as the murder weapon," he said, "it'd have sediment particles floating in it."

"We'd have to check with Rosamel, but yes, I think that's the case."

Mac nodded. "It's a long shot but what do we have to lose. I'm going to see if the CSI team can use that information." He regarded her. "That's good thinking." Then he grinned. "'I have surrounded myself with very smart people.'"

"Thanks," she said as she felt the heat rise to her cheeks. "More Robert Burns?"

With an impish smile, he shook his head. "Dolly Parton." He stood up. "I'm going to have to call that in ASAP." He extended his hand to her and helped her to stand. His touch lingered just a fraction of a second too long before he let her hand go. "We're going to be fighting time on it."

"I completely understand," she said, despite being disappointed their time together was ending. "I've got to get back to the B&B."

"All right," he said, as they both headed to the parking lot. He took out his phone. "I'll let you know if we come up with anything."

As he stopped next to the sheriff's SUV, he gave her a smile and a wave. She did the same before going back to her car.

21

Back at the B&B, once the chores were done, Maris and Cookie headed toward the back of the house and their rooms. Since the public areas didn't have to be cleaned every day, this morning's duties had been a little lighter.

"I think I'll change and then see how the little plantlings are doing before the greenhouse gets warm," Cookie said.

"Sounds like a plan," Maris said. "You gotta watch those kids."

Cookie chuckled. "Don't want them to get out of hand." She paused where they parted ways. "How about you?"

"I think I'll tidy my room," Maris lied. "Maybe wrangle a few dust bunnies."

The chef nodded. "Don't want them to get

out of hand either." With that, they went to their rooms and closed the doors.

Mojo was lounging on the bed, looking his usual relaxed and content self. He wasn't one to always seek out attention, but Maris adored the fact that, when he got it, he was always pleased. As she stroked the soft fur at the sides of his face using both her hands, his big orange eyes looked up at her.

"Ready for another visit?"

Though she might eventually chase down some dust balls, she had other priorities at the moment. Encouraged by her ability to descend into the cellars at Alegra Winery, she felt more than up to the challenge of the basement today.

As if in answer to her question, Mojo jumped from the bed and went to the utility room door at the back of her bedroom.

She smiled as she took the large black skeleton key from the hook next to the bedroom door. "I'll take that as a yes."

Nose to the door, he answered with his signature meow. When she opened it, he trotted directly to the hatch in the floor that led down to the basement. He sat down on it, right next to the lock.

"You're really ready today," she said to him as she slid the large metal key into the clunky mechanism and turned it. Despite feeling upbeat about doing better with her mild claustrophobia, the sound of the heavy metal gears sent a small shiver down her spine.

"You're on a roll," she muttered. "Don't stop now."

Finally the key turned freely and she grasped the handle. She glanced at Mojo who hadn't moved. "You're about to go for a ride if you don't get off." But in response he only stared at her hand on the handle. "Suit yourself."

Slowly, she lifted the hatch. Though Mojo sat still for a moment or two, he quickly leapt down to the floor and peered into the darkness below. As soon as there was room to maneuver, he zoomed down the stairs. Maris pushed the hatch open and rested it on the floor.

Despite feeling pretty confident when she'd come in, the view down the dark stairs gave her pause. If only she had the same great nighttime vision that Mojo had. Compared to the basement, the cellar at Alegra had been well lit.

"That's it," she said. Maybe she just needed more light.

She went down the few steps that it took to reach below the floor and flipped on the light switch. When the long fluorescent lights came on, it was better—and more familiar each time. Along the left wall was the diagonal bookcase that paralleled the stairs. The soft sheen of the leather spines tempted her to pause and look through the antique books that Glenda had collected. Though she'd found some interesting information on magic in them—and they had always been worth her time—today she had a different goal in mind.

She took another few steps down.

More bookcases down below were filled with piles of magazines as well as more books, mostly cloth hardbacks. An antique chest of drawers sat against the wall, topped with an old leather suitcase covered with faded stickers. Next to that was a column of hatboxes.

In her periodic exercises to go further and further down the stairs, she'd already made it to the floor once and even rescued a toppling hat box. This time, she needed to venture even further. But as she forced herself to slowly take the last few steps, she realized it was different from the winery. In the wine cellar, she hadn't been alone. She'd also been distracted by conversation, not to mention Mac. Here, all she had were her own thoughts.

"I'm thinking good thoughts," she said, "positive ones. Thoughts about wide open spaces." First one foot landed on the basement floor, then the other. "Great thoughts about exploring." She moved toward the hat boxes. "Of finding new things." Her gaze fell on a large plastic storage bin on the floor next to them. "Which is ironic, of course. Since this place is full of old things."

She knew what she was doing. It was the verbal equivalent of whistling past the graveyard. She was going to talk herself into being brave, even as the familiar tightening in her chest wound up.

"Who knows, maybe I'll even find the green pendulum."

It'd been the original reason she'd come down here in the first place. Conspicuous by its absence from Aunt Glenda's pretty bro-cade box, Maris had searched high and low, inside and out, under and over. The base-ment had been the only place left to carry on the search. But if she were actually going to stand a chance of finding it, she'd need to spend more than three seconds at a time down here.

At that moment, Mojo came trotting back to her. He lightly scratched the storage bin.

"That looks as good a place as any," she said to him, quickly grasping the lid. She would pull it off, look inside, put it back on, and bound back up the stairs to the first floor. It wouldn't take more than a minute. "Let's see what we've got." She grasped the edges of the dusty lid. "If this ends up being another one of your toys, I'm going to stop opening bins and boxes." She lifted the lid away—and could hardly believe what she saw. "Ha!" she said, putting aside the lid. "It isn't one of your toys. It's one of mine." She picked up the col-orful if well-worn box. "Monopoly," she murmured.

It was the game that she had played as a kid when she'd visited the B&B. She opened the top and lifted the folded board. There was the money, the property cards, the tokens, and everything, even both dice. Although Mojo had got up on his hind legs to look over the edge, apparently nothing interested him. He didn't jump in, look around at any of the other crates, or try to knock the hat boxes over. Instead he went back to the stairs and started up.

Maris quickly closed the game and put the lid on the storage box. "Hey," she said, tucking the board game under her arm. "Wait for me."

She trotted up after him. As he went into her bedroom, she closed and locked the hatch. Only when she gazed down at the closed wooden door did she realize what she'd done. Though a trickle of sweat ran down her back and she had to wipe her forehead with the back of her hand, she smiled. She'd actually distracted herself long enough to do a little investigating down there.

She was definitely making progress.

By the time she went into her room, Mojo had climbed back on the bed and sprawled comfortably. When she gave his head a scratch, he looked up at the sound of the tokens and dice rattling inside the game box.

"I'm going to put this in the parlor," she said. "You take your nap."

As she continued to stroke his head, his eyes dutifully shut, and she quietly slipped out.

22

As Maris headed to the parlor, she imagined guests enjoying the board game. Although this particular version was the classic type from her childhood, she knew that special editions existed. For a moment she wondered if there was one for wine regions, maybe Napa or France. She grinned a little at the thought. Instead of houses and hotels, there'd be vineyards and wineries. Alegra Winery might be a high priced property in her version of the game, while Crown might be more average.

She was about to head into the parlor, when she heard a noise from the kitchen. Cookie had said she was heading outside. Had one of the guests returned?

As she moved toward the sound, she

glanced down the hallway to the front entry. There didn't appear to be any cars in the driveway. She'd also just left Mojo in her bedroom.

Without meaning to be sneaky, she tread softly and held the game still so it wouldn't make noise. She came to a silent stop and peeked through the kitchen door.

It was Cookie—and she was trying Delia's hot sauce on one of her homemade tortillas.

"Ahem," Maris said, stepping in.

Cookie didn't even flinch, let alone jump. Instead she calmly turned around, saw who it was, and took another bite. Then she nodded. "I've got to admit," she said, showing Maris the bottle. "These really are wonderful."

Maris did a double take when she looked at the hot sauce Cookie had chosen. "Delia's Scorching Smokehouse? That's the nuclear one!"

The older woman only shook a few more drops onto the tortilla. "I can see why it's Eugene's favorite." She took a bite.

Maris was ready to run for the hose or a glass of milk or maybe even creamer, but the chef only nodded again. "Excellent balance of spice, heat, and flavor. That woman really has a talent." She eyed what Maris was carrying. "What have you got there?"

Though Maris was still staring at the tortilla, she held the game forward. "I found this in the basement. I was thinking that maybe our guests would enjoy playing it."

Cookie came closer for a better look. "Oh, Monopoly. Goodness, yes. I haven't seen that for years." She smiled at Maris. Apparently smoke wasn't going to start pouring out of Cookie's ears. "Do you remember playing that with Glenda?"

Maris grinned at her. "Remember? As I recall she was usually the real estate mogul left at the end."

Cookie laughed. "She was that indeed."

"Making loans on outrageous terms," Maris recalled.

"Ugh," Cookie said, rolling her eyes. "You had to take out the trash for a week."

"And you had to make caramel fudge brownies," Maris replied. "My favorite—and hers too."

"The woman was positively ruthless," the chef said, smiling.

Maris gazed down at the game. It felt

good to remember Glenda like this. Nor was it hard to picture her because, now that Maris was older, she was almost her spitting image. The trip to the basement had been well worth braving the confined space. Then she remembered her idea.

"I was just thinking that a winery version of it would be fun. Maybe have vineyards and wineries, instead of houses and hotels. And the tokens might be grapes or bottles or wine glasses."

"Or a corkscrew," Cookie suggested, "or maybe a barrel."

"Now you're talking," Maris said. She looked at the box top. "I think the utilities would be the same but the railroads..."

"Maybe flower farms instead," Cookie said.

Maris grinned at her. "I think we're on to something here. If it doesn't already exist, we need to make a winery version."

"Speaking of wineries," Cookie said, dribbling even more hot sauce on the last bit of tortilla. "I wonder how Rosamel is doing."

Maris thought for a moment. "I didn't see her at the winery this morning." Then she recalled the precognitive vision she'd had of

Rosamel among the vines. "Maybe I should pay another visit and check in on her."

Cookie smiled. "I'm sure she'd appreciate that."

"All right," Maris said, hefting the board game. "I'll just put this in the parlor, and make a trip to the winery."

"I'm heading out to the greenhouse," Cookie said. "For real this time." She popped the tortilla in her mouth. "Good stuff," she murmured.

23

After Maris parked in the lot, she didn't head to the winery itself. In her brief vision, she'd seen Rosamel among the vines. Nor had she been with any volunteers or workers. So Maris struck out in a direction that seemed to match the background of the precognitive image. The land had been fairly flat, not the gently rolling terrain that bordered the back of the crushing room. The late morning sun was high and bright, casting black shadows onto the dark, rich soil. As Maris walked up the row of vines, she inhaled the earthy scent and the woody aroma of the plants.

Cookie would enjoy this, she thought.

The further she got from the winery, the

more it seemed like she was visiting an entirely different country. She let her fingers trail along the large leaves on the vines, and also the unpicked, dark-skinned fruit. They felt like so many little pebbles, no doubt ready to burst.

At the end of the row, she stepped into a dirt lane that seemed to separate two fields of plants. She looked one way and then the other, as though she was crossing the street, and caught some movement out of the corner of her eye. It was Rosamel, in the distance. How far she'd come, Maris didn't know, but any sound of the winery or cars on the roads had faded. Even so, rather than call out to her, Maris simply went up the lane.

As she approached, she could see that the young woman was doing something. Although she was proceeding slowly up a row of vines, she was staring down at the ground. Only when Maris reached that row did she see that the winemaker was holding a small branch. It was in the shape of a Y and she was holding it by the wide end, pointing the longest stem at the ground.

If Maris hadn't known better, she'd say

Rosamel was dowsing—searching for underground water with the stick.

"Good morning," Maris said. With a tiny shriek, Rosamel jumped and whirled at the same time. "Sorry!" Maris held up both hands. "I didn't mean to sneak up on you."

"Whoa," Rosamel gasped, putting a hand to her chest. "I didn't hear you coming."

"I was just enjoying the quiet," Maris said. "Next time I'll shout."

Rosamel patted her breastbone and smiled. "I'm not normally so easy to scare," she said. Then realized she was holding the dowsing rod, and put it behind her back. "I guess I was...lost in thought." She gazed at Maris, and then back at the winery in the distance. "Are you looking for me?"

"I am," Maris said. "I just wanted to check and see how you're doing."

"Oh," Rosamel said, sounding relieved. "That's so nice of you. Thanks." She relaxed and Maris saw her shoulders slump. "I guess I'm doing okay. You know, considering everything."

"Of course," Maris said. "I know it can't be easy."

Then the young woman tilted her head, and stared at Maris. "How did you know to look for me out here?"

Maris smiled and gestured around them. "You might say that I think it's sort of a...*magical* setting." She watched Rosamel for any reaction, but the young woman's expression was guarded. "You might even say that in such a setting, it might not be too shocking for magical people to come across one another."

"Oh?" the young woman said. Realization seemed to dawn on her face, quickly followed by astonishment. "Oh!" She brought the dowsing rod out from behind her back. "Um, yeah. I guess that wouldn't be too shocking, would it?"

Maris smiled at her. "No, it wouldn't, which is my roundabout answer of how I knew you'd be out here."

Rosamel regarded her. "Huh. Very interesting."

"Looking for water?" Maris asked, pointing to the rod.

For a moment, the young woman hesitated but then she held up the stick. "I inherited the water dowsing ability from my mother. My father had a magical tasting ability—like down to the molecule."

"Ah," Maris said, nodding. "That would account for the winery's gold medals right from the start." She gazed around at the vineyard. "And let me guess. You had a hand in selecting the site."

Rosamel nodded. "But to give my father his due, he was a wonderful vintner. Just because you can identify a taste doesn't mean you can create something good." She shrugged. "But I'm sure it helped."

"Oh, of course," Maris quickly agreed. "All the magic in the world doesn't help you if you don't already have some talent." She looked at the rod. "Are you thinking of expanding? Maybe adding more fields?"

"Oh no," she said, shaking her head. Despite the fact that they were alone and a hundred yards from anyone, Rosamel looked behind her and lowered her voice. "I'm trying to get to the bottom of this claim of Friedrich Krone's that we're stealing his water."

So Maris wasn't the only person he'd told. She wondered if he'd brought it up with Dom.

She took a step closer. "And what have you found?"

"Quite the opposite." The young woman used the rod to point along the path to the winery. "Our winery is perfectly within its water rights. No worries there." Then she pointed in the opposite direction. Maris realized they were looking at the stone castle of Crown Winery in the distance. "But the water table beneath Crown is definitely dwindling, very likely due to the Pixie Petal Farms on its other side."

"So Friedrich is right, but he's got the wrong culprit."

"The wrong culprit?" Rosamel said, her face turning stern. "First, I would guess that they're within their water rights too. The water tables might be linked or even the same, and I wouldn't be surprised if they're using more water as their business grows. But second, as far as a culprit, there's only one that I can see." She angrily shook the dowsing rod at the ground. "It looks to me like someone at Crown Winery is drilling diagonal wells to get to the water table under our property." She pointed an accusing finger at the gray castle. "They're the ones stealing water."

Maris shaded her eyes with her hand, gazing in that direction. Then she turned back to Rosamel. "What do you say to paying them a visit?"

After parking, Maris followed a fast-walking Rosamel through the unfamiliar winery. The young woman never hesitated, as though she knew her way around. As they approached the crushing room, Maris recognized the sound of the giant machine. Crown Winery was indeed busy with its own harvest.

Workers at the conveyor belt in the back were moving quickly to remove the largest twigs and other debris before the forklift took the plastic bins of fruit to the crusher. But one young man in particular stood out, literally head and shoulders above the rest. He looked up from his work, just as Rosamel and Maris approached.

"Rosamel!" he said, as he nearly dropped

the empty plastic bin he was carrying. His eyes were huge and his mouth hung open slightly. "What are you doing here?"

His deep voice was easily heard over the din, but Rosamel cupped her hands around her mouth and shouted, "We need to talk." She pointed to the already harvested vines behind him.

As they moved away from the din, Maris saw Harlan glance at her. "Harlan, we haven't been properly introduced." She extended her hand. "I'm Maris Seaver, and I run the Pixie Point Bay Lighthouse and B&B. Rosamel was giving me a tour of her harvesting operation when I first saw you."

Though he looked at her hand for a second, he finally took it and gave it a gentle shake. "You work with the sheriff?"

"From time to time," she answered. "I happened to be with Rosamel when she learned of her father's death."

Rosamel put a hand on Maris's shoulder. "She was with me when I went to the cellar and saw him."

Harlan's worried expression seemed to clear. "Oh, I see. Then you have my–"

"Uh oh," Rosamel said.

Maris turned to see Friedrich approaching them. His face was twisted into an ugly scowl.

"What is she doing here?" he shouted, as Harlan quickly moved Rosamel behind him.

"She's with me," Maris said, holding up a hand. "This was my idea."

"I don't care whose idea it was," the wine-maker raged, his face red. He jabbed a finger in her direction. "She's not welcome here."

Before Harlan could stop her, Rosamel popped out from behind him. "I'll bet I'm not," she shouted. "But my water is." Hands balled into fists, Friedrich stared at her, as though trying to comprehend her words. Now she pointed at him. "You heard me, water thief." She looked up at Harlan. "Your father has been digging diagonal wells into my land."

Harlan backed up from her, the shock plain in his face. "What?"

She crossed her arms over her chest and thrust her chin out at Friedrich. "Ask him."

Harlan slowly turned to his father. "What's this about?"

The older man's lips pressed together in a thin white line and his eyes narrowed to slits.

"You'd take her side?" Although Harlan looked like he was about to answer, Friedrich cut him off with a wave of his hand and glared at Rosamel. "Get out." She looked like she wanted to say something too, but Friedrich was having none of it. "Get out!" he bellowed at the top of his lungs. "Get out!"

Maris almost had to cover her ears at the strident sound. Quickly, she went to Rosamel and grabbed her arm. Without a word, she dragged her back toward the building, and was relieved to find that the young woman hardly resisted. Although the crusher was still running, all work had stopped as everyone stared at them.

This had been a bad idea.

"Let's go," Maris said, and led Rosamel out of the crushing room.

It was another fast walk back to the lobby and then the parking lot, but this time Maris took the lead.

"He didn't deny it," Rosamel said, breathing hard. "Did you see that? He didn't deny it. He couldn't."

"I saw," Maris said, unlocking the doors on her car. "And I heard." They both got in, Maris started the engine, and locked the doors. "The next time that I suggest we go anywhere and confront a tall, volatile man about water rights, it's okay to say no." She strapped on her seat belt, as Rosamel did the same.

"It was worth it, though," the young woman said. "The look on his face made it worth it."

As Maris backed the car out, she saw a familiar red SUV in the rear view mirror. Charlie was here. Apparently the gift of the magnums had worked.

Then she recalled the mottled red rage that had swept over Friedrich Krone's face. Now she had to wonder about whether or not he really could have killed Dom. As she imagined the tall man wielding a bottle of wine, a shiver of cold ran down her core. She quickly put the car in drive.

This really had been a bad idea.

25

By the time Maris got home, she'd managed to calm down and think things through. As she parked the car she realized it didn't make sense. If Friedrich Krone was stealing water, then what was his motive for murder? If anything, it'd be Alegra Winery holding the grudge, not Crown.

Harlan had said nothing, not that there'd been much opportunity. But he'd said very little to Mac as well. What was he not telling them about his meeting with Dom? Did he share the same bad temper as his father? Perhaps the Krones had arranged a business deal with Charlie Gorian, acing out Rosamel now that her father was dead.

Maris shook her head. As usual, there

were too many questions and not enough an-swers. But as she gazed out the windshield to the B&B and lighthouse rising behind it, she remembered that she had another means of investigation of which she'd yet to avail her-self: the Old Girl.

With a new sense of purpose, she got out of the car and headed to the back of the prop-erty, down the side. Like all the lightkeepers before her, Maris shared a special bond with Claribel. Not only did the Old Girl hold the North American record for most boats saved, she was a magical being—the former no doubt helped by the latter.

Cookie must have finished in the green-house, since both it and the garden were empty. As Maris approached on the lawn, an invisible ocean breeze swirled around her, blowing her skirt and hair. As she moved her bangs from her eyes she smiled. The door to the lighthouse blew open and she stepped through.

"Good morning, Claribel," Maris said, and turned on the light.

At this time of day, she didn't really need the extra illumination, but it was a habit. The windows at each level of the lighthouse not only looked out on different beautiful views, they let in plenty of sun. As she climbed the spiraling, wrought iron staircase, Maris first looked out to the bay. Its pristine waters glittered like a rounded pool filled with dark sapphires. At the second level, the view was to the south, along the coast. The undulating seashore met the ocean with its own earthy hues of buff cliffs backed by verdant green hills. Finally at the third level, and just before reaching the top, the view was over the roof of the B&B. Beyond the lush hills and the town of Pixie Point Bay, the mountains with their redwood forests rose in green and purple tones. Each window's view could have been a postcard, including looking down on the many gabled Victorian lightkeeper's home that was now a B&B.

Breathing a little hard, Maris finally climbed up the last step onto the metal floor of the optical room. This spot was where the views all came together, and she never tired of seeing the seamless panorama. If Pixie Point Bay was magical, then this part of the coast, the Middle Kingdom, was simply enchanted. It felt as though you could see for hundreds of miles in every direction as land, sea, and sky flowed from one to another, horizon to horizon. She took a moment to catch her breath and take in the view—but just a moment. She had not come up the three story tower for the grand vista.

Instead she turned to the fresnel lens that was the all-seeing eye of the lighthouse. More like a sculpture of crystal clear glass segments mounted on a gleaming steel frame, the entire thing was taller than her with an overall egg shape. Many of the pieces of glass were etched with fine concentric circles, each of them throwing out tiny rainbow sparkles in every direction. As usual, Maris gazed into them, letting her eyes defocus and relax. She took in a slow breath and lightly blew it out, as the sparkles began to glow and then coalesce, until finally an image appeared.

It was Delia and Eugene.

"Hmm," Maris said, watching them. Like looking through a telescope, she saw them enlarged and up close. Both were wearing aprons emblazoned with the smokehouse logo, and their round faces were smiling. From the looks of what little background could be seen, it seemed as though they might be in a kitchen. Empty and unlabeled bottles of hot sauce stood by as Eugene put a funnel to the top of one, and Delia brought over a steaming sauce pan and tipped in some of the contents. Then he moved on to the next bottle, his daughter moving with him.

Suddenly, the image winked out.

Maris blinked. Though it had been quick, it had been clear. She'd been watching the Burnsides bottling their signature, home-made hot sauce—which made her frown a little.

What did their hot sauce have to do with Dom's murder, or even a winery? Or maybe it was more the father-daughter relationship she was supposed to focus on? She pursed her lips. Either way, staying in the lighthouse wasn't going to tell her why Claribel had shown that to her.

She gave the glass base of the lens a gentle pat. "Thanks, Old Girl. Much appreciated, as always."

It was time to pay the Smokehouse another visit.

26

"Maris," Eugene said, grinning from behind the hostess stand. "It's great to see you again so soon." He brought out a menu and offered it to her.

She held up a hand. "I won't be needing that today," she said, smiling.

"A woman who knows what she wants," Eugene said, hugging the menu to his big belly. "What can I get for you?"

On her way into town, Maris had decided to take home more hot sauces. Apart from being a good excuse for the visit, they really were excellent.

"One of each of your wonderful hot sauces," she replied.

"Ah," he said nodding, with a look of supreme satisfaction. "Another convert."

"A couple, actually," she replied. "Cookie was really impressed with the nuclear version."

His eyes twinkled. "My favorite. And if Cookie likes it..." He pumped his fist. "That's the kind of seal of approval we're looking for." He put away the menu. "One of each, it is. Delia will be thrilled. I'll be right back."

"Actually," Maris said, stopping him, "if you have a minute, could I ask you a question?"

"Well, it's my lucky day," he said, turning back to her. "What's on your mind?"

She glanced at the swinging metal door to the kitchen. "Do you make the sauces here?"

The older man nodded. "In fact, we do. Absolutely. Just Delia and I, right in that kitchen."

Maris regarded him. "Just the two of you? Isn't that a lot of work?"

He shrugged. "It is, but it's safer that way."

"Safer?" Maris said, thinking about what Cookie had said about not touching her eyes if she touched the hot sauce. "Do you mean from the steam, maybe?"

Eugene laughed. "Oh no. We can take the steam." He waggled his eyebrows at her. "Otherwise we'd have to stay out of the kitchen." He shook his head. "No, what I'm talking about is security."

"Security," she said, her brows furrowing. "I'm afraid you've lost me."

He leaned in and lowered his voice. "Last year, we found someone on the internet trying to sell our sauces—except we're the only ones who sell them."

Maris thought about it. "Maybe someone who bought some here?"

Eugene shook his head. "They were shipping cases of it."

"Cases?" Maris exclaimed. "Then what were they doing?"

The older man ran his thumbs behind his suspenders, up and down. "Counterfeiters were making fake sauce."

"Counterfeiters? Fake sauce?" she said, sounding like an echo chamber, even to herself. But it was a little hard to imagine—particularly if Eugene and Delia were fire elementals, as Cookie had guessed. How could anyone reproduce what they did?

"It all ended fine though," Eugene said, nodding.

"Really? How?"

"They don't know our recipe—not that it would help them if they did." He gave her a wink.

"So it was their own recipe with your labels on it?"

"Not exactly," he said, scoffing. "They actually had some samples of our sauces. But they were just mixing other sauces together, trying to get lucky and get the same taste." He shook his head and smiled. "They're lucky we didn't call the police. Just a legal letter or two and it was done."

"Wow," Maris said. "So they didn't even try to cook."

Eugene smirked. "Probably didn't know how. They couldn't even get the labels right."

Suddenly she thought of the wine tasting at the B&B. She frowned a little at the memory. It had nothing to do with hot sauces. Or did it?

"I'm talking your ear off today," Eugene said, turning to go. "Let me get that order for you."

When he'd gone, she gave her temple a

discreet tap. She looked at each of the tasting bottles in turn. But it was the final Bordeaux that held her interest. But why? She'd already alerted Mac to the sediment issue. No, it had to be something else.

Prior to the tasting she'd done a bunch of internet research and had run across many of the most expensive Bordeauxs that existed. Now she compared one in particular to one in her memory. Then she looked at the auction catalog information about it.

"Ah ha," she muttered.

Just then Eugene returned with a little brown to-go bag. Quickly she removed her wallet, took out cash, and laid it on the podium. "Thank you, Eugene. You've been a huge help."

"Always a pleasure," he said, handing her the bag. He picked up the cash. "But–"

She was already heading out the door. "Gotta make a phone call," she said over her shoulder. "Thanks!"

27

The dining room of the B&B was not only full, it was tense. Maris stood at the end of the table nearest the window, while Mac stood at the opposite end near the door. Seated on one side were Rosamel and Charlie. On the other were Harlan and his father. The elder Krone was already glowering at everyone, especially the sheriff. But Mac seemed not to notice.

He tossed a manila folder to the table. "The Medio County forensics team has, I'm glad to report, found a needle in a needle factory." He smiled as he looked at each of the attendees. Then he nodded to Maris. "But I'll get to that as soon as Maris is done."

Every head swiveled to her, almost as one, as though they were at a tennis match. But she addressed her first remark to the sheriff. "It would appear that Crown Winery has been digging diagonal wells into the water table below Alegra Winery."

Rosamel stiffened, her wide eyes staring at Maris. If the young woman was worrying about her magic ability coming to light, she needn't have. There was no need to reveal it. But the fact that it was happening needed to be addressed.

Friedrich's fist pounded the table. "The water was stolen from my property in the first place."

Harlan placed his big hand on his father's arm. "Dad," was all he said. But when Friedrich tried to shake him off, Maris watched as the young man slowly tightened his grip. "That's enough." When his father finally looked at him, Harlan let go. He gazed up at Mac. "I'll be looking into that."

"I think you'll find," Rosamel said to him, "that your water loss is due to the Pixie Point Petal flower farms adjoining your property. Their rapidly increasing acreage is putting a dent in the water table."

"When it comes to water rights," Mac

said, "you're going to need to get a USGS survey."

Harlan nodded. "I'm already working on it."

"But really, Mr. Krone," Maris said to Friedrich. "It wasn't the water that had you boiling mad that day when I was visiting Alegra Winery."

The older man jutted out his lower lip, crossed his arms over his chest, and glared at the table. While Maris simply looked at him, perfectly willing to wait him out, his son turned to him.

"Just tell them the truth, Dad," he said quietly. "It'll be all right."

But Friedrich only pursed his lips.

"You couldn't have been that mad at Dominic Alegra," Maris said. "After all, you shared a glass of wine with him."

"Hmph," Friedrich said. Then he glared at her. But when Harlan elbowed him, he said, "I had no issue with the man himself."

"Then what had you mad that day?" Mac asked.

"Him!" Friedrich shouted, jerking a thumb at his son.

Mac motioned for him to keep the

volume down. "We can all hear you, Mr. Krone."

"He's been sneaking away from our winery for *months*," the older man spat. "I'm sick of it."

"In fact," Maris said, "he was at Alegra that morning." Rosamel exchanged a look with Maris, while Friedrich glared at her. "What were you discussing with Dominic when Charlie arrived and saw the two of you together?"

Harlan looked at Charlie, who smiled sheepishly and shrugged.

Friedrich and Rosamel, however, both whipped their heads around to stare at the younger Krone.

"You were with my father?" Rosamel said, leaning forward and putting both of her hands flat on the table. "That morning?" She stared at Maris, who nodded, and then back at Harlan. "And you didn't tell me?"

"Conspiring with him," Friedrich said, his voice tight. His eyes quickly shut, and his jaw muscles clenched. Maris even thought she heard his teeth grinding. "How could you?"

Harlan ignored him and gazed back at

Rosamel. Impossibly, he was even smiling. "I asked him for your hand in marriage."

Friedrich's eyes snapped open and blinked several times before he stared open-mouthed at his son.

Rosamel sat back hard in her chair, her jaw dropped almost to her chest.

Mac's eyebrows shot up and he exchanged a look with Maris, who only grinned.

"Wow," Charlie whispered.

Harlan continued to smile at Rosamel. "We've been secretly seeing each other since the summer. Finally, I knew I'd met my forever girl. So I popped the question, and she said yes." Maris glanced at Rosamel to see her flushing a deep red. "We were going to elope. We knew that neither of our parents was going to be pleased." Harlan reached out both his hands across the table, and Rosamel immediately took them. "But I saw how much it bothered you that your father didn't know. So I went to him, man to man, and simply told him the truth. And you know what?" Rosamel could only shake her head. "He was happy for us." Harlan squeezed her hands. "That's how much he loved you."

Rosamel burst into tears. "Oh my god," she gasped. She had to cover her face with her hands. "Oh my god."

Harlan looked up at Maris, his eyes misty too. "We were toasting the engagement when Charlie arrived."

Maris fetched a box of tissues from the sideboard and set it in front of Rosamel.

"Thank you," she sniffed.

When Maris resumed her position, she and Mac both turned their gazes toward Charlie. The young wine investor was smiling at Harlan, and then realized with a start that they were looking at him. He cleared his throat.

"The special wine that you uncorked for my guests the other night," Maris said to him. "The 1971 Clos St. Denis Grand Cru?"

"*Another* rare Bordeaux?" Friedrich said.

"I never leave home without them," Charlie said to him, grinning. He looked at Maris. "I think everyone enjoyed it."

Maris regarded him. "They enjoyed something, but it wasn't a 1971 Clos St. Denis Grand Cru because, according to my research, Domaine Ponsot didn't start bottling it until 1982."

Still smiling, Charlie shook his head. "There are many Bordeaux wineries, many varietals, and many vintages. It's easy to get confused. I can assure you that we did indeed taste the 1971 Grand Cru—from my private collection."

"I can assure you," Maris said, her tone light, "that I haven't made a mistake."

To that, Charlie only shrugged, as though he preferred not to argue.

Mac picked up the manila folder. "All of the fingerprints from the cellar have come back." He glanced down at the top sheet. "Mr. Alegra's prints were there, along with both the Krones, and also Mr. Gorian's."

"Of course," Charlie said, glancing at Harlan and Friedrich. "I guess we were all drinking wine there."

"Ah," the sheriff said. "But here is where the needle in the needle factory comes in. The crime scene investigation unit first paid particular attention to any bottles in the cellar that were free of dust. That actually eliminated the majority of the collection down there."

"It's there to age," Rosamel said. "They should all have some amount of dust."

"Exactly," Mac agreed. "But a few did not."

"Dom might have been examining them," Harlan suggested. "Or maybe showing them."

"But probably not cleaning them," the sheriff said.

Harlan nodded to that, and Friedrich snorted. "You shouldn't touch them. He would have known that."

Mac looked back at the papers in the folder. "But for the bottles that were relatively free of dust, the team used a high intensity light to examine them in place without disturbing them. Only one had sediment floating in the wine." The sheriff gazed around the table. "It was almost entirely free of dust, and the sediment had been disturbed because the bottle had been moved."

"The murder weapon," Maris said.

"Right," Mac said. "It had been wiped clean. No traces of hair or blood."

Rosamel flinched, and Harlan held out a hand, which she took.

"So no fingerprints either," Friedrich said. "Even though you found the weapon."

The sheriff held up one finger. "Except for one. In the curved bottom of the bottle, right in the center, there was a partial thumb print."

Charlie started to stand, but Mac went to his chair and put a hand on his shoulder. "Please remain seated, Mr. Gorian."

"I think everyone here," Maris began, "acknowledges Dominic's incredible palate, even you, Charlie." Though he looked at her, he didn't say anything. "In fact, his sense of taste was so good, that he knew your 1947 St-Emilion was a fake. That's why he spit it out."

"A fake?" Friedrich whispered. Then he grimaced. "No wonder he let me take it." He glanced at Mac. "I saved the bottle."

"Dominic had you figured out," Maris said. "Didn't he Charlie?" His smile was gone now. "And then you had to protect your investment."

In answer, he only shrugged again.

Mac took him by the arm and helped him to stand. "Wine fraud is a multi-million dollar business," the sheriff said, as he took the handcuffs from his utility belt. "But you won't be going to jail for fraud, Mr. Gorian. You are under arrest for the murder of Dominic Alegra."

28

At the Alegra Winery tasting room, Maris watched Rosamel pour. The large pink solitaire of her engagement ring sparkled, even under the recessed lights.

"Hey, Boss," said one of the servers. "We're running low on napkins and olives."

Rosamel nodded toward the exit. "In the storeroom, at the back, on the right for the napkins. Next to the door on the second shelf for the olives."

No sooner did the server leave, than another employee showed up. "Boss, there's someone on the phone about the barrels."

Rosamel finished pouring. "Get a name and number and tell them I'll call them back within the hour."

As yet another employee showed up with a question, Maris had a moment to think back on Mojo's tarot clue: The Magician. He was a man of magic, to be sure, but he was also known as a trickster. In fact, in the most sinister of modern interpretations, you could call him a con man. That title suited Charlie Gorian to a tee. He'd taken them all in.

Mojo's Ouija clue of "wine" had been spot on as well. Yes, the murder had taken place in a winery, and the murder weapon had been a wine bottle, but it turned out that the motive for the murder had been wine as well. She had to smile to herself and silently thanked the little cat, although she'd be even more appreciative for a little more detail in the future.

Eventually, Rosamel seemed to get a break. As the young woman slid the glass over, Maris accepted it with a smile. "It seems you've really taken over the reins. Good for you."

Dom's funeral had only been a few days ago, and Maris had decided to wait to pick up her wine since the B&B was stocked for the time being. But it seemed that the shock of her father's death was waning, no doubt aided by the busyness of the harvest season.

"Well, there's been a little help in that department," Rosamel said. Her face lit up as she nodded to something behind Maris. She turned to find Harlan, in an Alegra Winery shirt, approaching them. "He's been wanting to take over vintner duties for years."

He quickly went behind the counter and gave his fiancé a peck on the cheek. There had to be almost a two foot difference in height between them, and yet Maris had never seen a couple more well suited to one another.

"Maris," he said, "it's good to see you. I hope my partner here is treating you well."

"Partner?" she said, eying the shirt. "In life, or in business?"

He put his arm around Rosamel's shoulders. "Both. We're thinking of merging the two wineries eventually."

"Really," Maris said. "Is your father on board with that?"

Harlan grinned. "Not yet, but he will be. He just needs a little time."

"He's a good man," Rosamel added. "But change is hard."

Maris nodded. "Agreed, on both counts."

She lifted her glass. "May I be the first to toast your new adventure?"

Harlan quickly poured two more glasses. "By all means," he said.

With grins all around, Maris clinked her glass to theirs. "To the Alegra Crown Winery. May its magical wine-making never end."

"To the Alegra Crown Winery," the happy couple said.

As Maris sipped her wine, she decided it was easily the very best she'd ever tasted.

The Witch Who Saved the Bay

Excerpt

CHAPTER ONE

Maris Seaver lifted her sign as high as she could. "Go away, not this bay!" she chanted, along with the rest of the crowd. "Go away, not this bay!"

Although the weather at the Pixie Point Bay Pier was as clear and temperate as ever, the mood of the protestors was decidedly foul. No fishermen dropped their lines into the pristine waters, and no one was perusing the catch of the day. Instead the long wharf was filled with the townspeople of Pixie Point

Bay. As Maris started her second loop, she neared the reason for the protest: the two representatives of North American Petroleum.

The oil company had long made known its desire to place an oil derrick in the bay. Maris could remember Aunt Glenda and Cookie talking about it at mealtime when she was a child. It seemed inconceivable to her that anyone would want to mar the beauty of such a picturesque scene. But it wasn't the drilling platform itself that had bothered Glenda, it was the possibility of an oil spill.

Imagine all the marine life gone, she'd said. *If it goes, we go.*

Her somber and worried tone had stuck with Maris all these years because, in the end, her aunt had been right. The longer that Maris lived here, the more she understood just how intertwined their lives were with the bay: from the fresh seafood for which the area was known, to the fishing economy, not to mention the tourism and visiting ships. Without all those boats, would there even be reason for a lighthouse?

Even if there's never a spill, Cookie had

said, *it'd be ugly. Can you imagine waking up to that every morning in your backyard?*

The longtime chef of the B&B had nailed it. Maris couldn't imagine it—or wouldn't.

"Please everyone," Audrey Graisser said through her megaphone. "Please, just let us have our say. This is a discussion, not a war."

In her mid-twenties, Audrey carried herself well. She wore her coppery red hair long, and her bright blue eyes always seemed to smile. She was dressed in a well-fitting gray business suit with a short skirt that showed off her pretty legs and figure. Though she seemed young for such a weighty job, Maris guessed she hadn't been picked for her vast experience. Her upbeat attitude and fresh face were completely winning. Despite understanding how cynical NAP had been when choosing her as a representative, Maris couldn't help but like her.

Though Audrey's companion was twice her age, he was equally charming. Joseph Toler, Esq., was no doubt on hand to make sure everything was done in compliance with regulations. He seemed to be able to recite them chapter and verse. His brunette hair was trimmed short and graying only at the sideburns. He smiled as much as Audrey, even surrounded by protestors, though his sea green eyes were alert. Like her, he was in business attire, but casual and without a tie.

He waved a hand above his head. "Please everyone," he shouted, "we'd just like to report on the EIR."

The environmental impact report, Maris thought. Everyone in town now knew what EIR meant. Audrey and Joseph had been here for a few days already, canvasing the businesses door-to-door, and trying to drum up support. Judging by today's rally, they'd had little success.

"Pipe down," a familiar voice called out. "*Pipe down.*"

Maris turned to see Slick standing on top of a wooden fish crate. The salty old seaman was waving his yellow slicker's hat. Despite the circumstances, she had to smile. Slick was a fixture on the pier. Day in and day out for decades, he kept the town supplied with the freshest and most varied seafood in this part of the world. As far as Maris was concerned, his long gray beard and leathery face only added to his charm. He'd been involved with her aunt, and now the two of them looked out for one another.

All around her his call for quiet was echoed. A few people murmured his name. When it came to the pier and the bay, Slick's word carried a lot of weight. As the chanting subsided, he said, "Let's not start a mutiny before the ship has set sail." Maris had to smirk.

He stepped down from the crate and held out a hand to Audrey, helping her to step up and take his place.

"Thank you, Captain Duff," she said, no longer using the megaphone. She handed it to Joseph. "And thank you all for being here." She smiled at many of the individuals she'd already met, including Maris. Both of the NAP representatives were staying at her B&B. "As many of you know, North American Petroleum is committed to the health and beauty of the bay."

Next to Maris, Howard Scry snorted, and she nodded her agreement to him. Owner of the Main Street Market, Howard bore an uncanny resemblance to Albert Einstein, only reinforced by the fact that he was a retired physics professor. "Beauty of the bay," he muttered, his white mustache twitching from side to side. "In a pig's eye."

Audrey breezily ignored the other similar rumblings from the crowd. "To that end, we have completed *two* independent EIRs." She waved a sheaf of papers in the air. "Copies of these are available right now." She indicated Joseph who began circulating through the crowd to hand them out. "Each of these companies has completed months of research and independently reported that any impact on the ecosystem of Pixie Point Bay would be nil."

Maris took a copy of the reports from Joseph as he passed by, as did Howard.

"Only if absolutely nothing went wrong," said Ryan Quigg. The young red head of Irish descent was not only the owner of the town's tackle shop, he was an avid fisherman. He was at the pier every morning. "What's the impact when there's a spill?"

"Yeah," someone else said. "What happens then?"

Audrey nodded. "I hear you. A spill would be a catastrophe. No doubt." She raised her voice a notch. "But let me remind you of North American Petroleum's track record." She made a circle with her finger and thumb. "Zero accidents." She paused for a moment. "Let me say that again. Zero. None. We're the company—and the only company I might add—with a perfect track record."

Though there were some shaking heads, no one contradicted her.

"It will be a complete and utter blight on the bay," Etienne Fournier said in his French accent. "Who is going to sit at my restaurant and look at such a monstrosity?" He waved his hand across the bay. "'And here is your wonderful view of metal.'" He shook his head. "No. I think not."

"And that is my second piece of good news today," Audrey said, looking at him. "North American Petroleum has decided to use a drillship, not an oil rig." Her smile was absolutely radiant. "You're not going to lose your wonderful view, Mr. Fournier. Your diners will simply see yet another ship in the bay."

Though Maris had never heard of a drillship, it didn't change the fact that liquid petroleum was going to be pumped from the bottom of the bay up to a waiting tanker. A massive industrial ship was a far cry from the luxury yachts and quaint sailboats that typically plied the waters. Nor did a perfect track record guarantee there wouldn't be an accident.

"And what about these documents?" a woman's voice said.

She was moving through the crowd, her hand high in the air with her own set of papers. All the townspeople recognized her as well. Like the NAP representatives, Julia Mendes had arrived early, and was also staying at the B&B. It'd made for a tense few days, but everyone had done their best to be civil—mostly by avoiding one another.

"Company emails," she said, as everyone parted for her. Someone patted her on the back. "Internal communication that makes it clear that the so-called 'independent' EIRs are anything but."

The petite brunette made her way to the front. Older than Audrey, Julia was still a young woman, thirty at most. It was due to her hard work that today's rally had been organized. She'd made the flyers and the signs, and had held several small meetings around Pixie Point Bay to clearly outline their goals and strategies. She was an environmental activist with an already impressive list of accomplishments from hot spots around the globe. From the moment she'd arrived, she'd appeared as passionate about the bay as the residents.

She took up position directly in front of Audrey, turned to the crowd, and shook her papers angrily over her head. "Those EIRs were done by companies with direct ties to NAP." Without looking at Audrey, she jabbed a finger at her. "Direct *financial* ties." She glared at the faces in the crowd, and took a copy of the EIRs from someone nearby. "They paid for these findings, pure and simple." She hurled the papers to the planks of the wharf. "If those EIRs were printed on softer paper, they might actually be useful."

Someone in the back of the crowd laughed. Someone else said, "It's all rigged."

"You can read it for yourselves," Julia shouted, shaking her printed emails. "They think we're going to roll over. They think we're already in their pocket."

Joseph had returned to the front as well. Audrey turned a troubled look to him. Clearly this was supposed to be his area.

"Hearsay," he said simply. He spread his hands. "I've never heard of these emails until now, and I'm not going to debate them without even seeing them."

"Here!" Julia shouted, shoving them at him. "Go ahead. No one's stopping you."

"What do they say?" Ryan shouted.

"Read it," Howard yelled.

But as Audrey darted pleading looks at Joseph, he simply smiled, crossed his arms, and shook his head. "That's not how it works. There are ways to falsify these types of documents. Someone will have to prove to me that these are real before I look at them."

Now Audrey scowled at him. She climbed down off the fish crate, and said something into his ear. As the shouting rose louder, he shook his head again.

Now it was the environmental activist who climbed onto the box. "Go away, not this bay! Go away, not this bay!"

Soon the chanting was up to full force. Joseph dragged Audrey away and soon Maris lost them in the crowd. Meanwhile Julia thrust her fists up into the air. "Yes! Victory for Pixie Point Bay!"

But just as Maris was going to join in the

chorus of hurrahs, she glanced across the bay. There, on the rocky promontory that jutted out into the water, the beam of her lighthouse flashed on and off.

"Uh oh," she said.

• • • • •

Buy The Witch Who Saved the Bay

DEDICATION

For Mr. Bee's Knees

COPYRIGHT

Copyright © 2020 Emma Belmont

This is a work of fiction. Names, characters, places, and incidents are products of the author's imagination or are used fictitiously and are not to be construed as real. Any resemblance to actual events, locales, organizations, or persons, living or dead, is coincidental.

All rights reserved. No part of this book may be used or reproduced in any manner, stored in or introduced into a retrieval system, or transmitted, in any form, or by any means (electronic, mechanical, photocopying, recording, or otherwise), without the prior written consent of the copyright owner.

The scanning, uploading, and distribution of this book via the Internet or via any other means without the permission of the copyright owner is illegal. Please purchase only authorized electronic editions, and do not participate in or encourage electronic piracy of copyrighted materials. Your support of the author's rights is appreciated.

www.ingramcontent.com/pod-product-compliance
Lightning Source LLC
Chambersburg PA
CBHW050512190726
48284CB00003B/784